"Far more than most dare admit, history and historians mix fact and fiction. The two were and are always inseparably intertwined. The 1871 Paris Commune—when a proletariat took political power from a bourgeoisie—transformed the social movement to do better than capitalism. Marx assessed the strengths and weaknesses of that transformative moment to advance that movement. Inspired by Marx's analysis, Lenin did likewise. This book adds to the tradition evolving since Marx and Lenin. Remarkably accessible, it refreshes, provokes, and thereby develops that movement still further."

—RICHARD WOLFF,
author of *Democracy at Work: A Cure for Capitalism*

"Michael Löwy and Olivier Besancenot 'discovered' a manuscript written by Karl Marx's daughter Jenny, revealing a secret visit of her father to Paris as it was besieged during the fateful weeks of the Commune. Their book is not an exercise in counter-factual history—a 'what if . . .'—but rather an original and inventive form of history writing. They describe the Commune by emphasizing its greatness, pointing out its limitations, and assessing its historical legacy in a pleasant and vigorous literary account. Thus, Marx dons the habit of a hidden observer who, along with the voice of his daughter, guides us through the labyrinth of a revolutionary experience in the making. Marx becomes a 'witness' and the Commune a living experience. This fictional account is a remarkable piece of historical criticism and revolutionary imagination."

—ENZO TRAVERSO,
author of *Revolution: An Intellectual History*

"The authors embarked on an imaginary visit to the Paris Commune, seen through the eyes of Karl Marx and his daughter Jenny, and the result is as true as real. Readers will learn more—and with great pleasure, at that—from reading this well-researched little book of historical fiction than they would learn from reading a thick academic volume."

—GILBERT ACHCAR,
author of *Marxism, Orientalism, Cosmopolitanism*

MARX IN PARIS
1871

JENNY'S "BLUE NOTEBOOK"

MICHAEL LÖWY
OLIVIER BESANCENOT

TRANSLATED BY TODD CHRETIEN

Haymarket Books
Chicago, Illinois

Published in 2022 by
Haymarket Books
P.O. Box 180165
Chicago, IL 60618
773-583-7884
www.haymarketbooks.org
info@haymarketbooks.org

ISBN: 978-1-64259-588-8

Distributed to the trade in the US through Consortium Book Sales
and Distribution (www.cbsd.com) and internationally through Ingram
Publisher Services International (www.ingramcontent.com).

This book was published with the generous support of Lannan
Foundation and Wallace Action Fund.

Special discounts are available for bulk purchases by organizations and
institutions. Please call 773-583-7884 or email info@haymarketbooks.
org for more information.

Cover design by Rachel Cohen.

Printed in Canada by union labor.

Library of Congress Cataloging-in-Publication data is available.

10 9 8 7 6 5 4 3 2 1

CONTENTS

INTRODUCTION

THE DISCOVERY OF JENNY MARX'S STRANGE "BLUE NOTEBOOK"

This is the story of how we came to be the improvised editors of Jenny Marx on one fine evening during the fall of 2019.

At the end of a meeting at la Bellevilloise in Paris, we ran into an old friend, Pierre Longuet, who proposed having a drink at a nearby bar. A distant descendant of Jenny Marx, Karl Marx's oldest daughter, and the Communard Charles Longuet, Pierre is very proud of his ancestors and loves regaling us with stories about them. We always enjoy hearing these tales—part family lore, part history, and occasionally a bit indiscreet. However, this time was different. As we drank our pints, he informed us of a curious discovery.

"The other day while rummaging around in an old trunk that belonged to my great-great-grandmother, filled with old books, some ankle boots, and an antediluvian sewing machine, I came across a large school notebook with a blue cover filled with notes in a fine, difficult-to-read handwriting. The first pages were particularly incomprehensible because they were written in Gothic German, in cursive. But I eventually figured out that it was written by my ancestor, and it was dated from the year 1871.

"Pierre, not to be too nosey, but could you show us the notebook? We would love to have a look."

"Why not? I hope you manage to decipher it."

Needless to say, our interest was piqued. We waited impatiently to get a look at our friend's treasure.

Sadly, little is known about Jenny Caroline Marx. She was born in 1844 and, by 1871, had become a socialist militant. In a posthumous tribute, Engels wrote that she was "a spirited and energetic presence, envied by many a man." She spoke fluent German, English, and French and helped support her parents with private language lessons. In 1870, she took the initiative to write two articles in *La Marsellaise*, a newspaper published by Henri Rochefort, signed under the pseudonym J. Williams, denouncing the treatment of Irish political prisoners in English prisons. The scandal was such that Prime Minister Gladstone was forced to free them some weeks later, allowing them to leave for the United States.

Franziska Kugelmann, the daughter of Marx's friend Ludwid Kugelmann, wrote a very sympathetic appreciation after Jenny's passing in 1881.

"Jenny Marx, a graceful and slender apparition in her black curls, closely resembled her father, both physically and morally. Cheerful, lively, and friendly, she abounded in grace and tact; anything gaudy or flamboyant was disagreeable to her."

Her mother recalled that Jenny "read widely, her horizons were very broad, and she was enthusiastic about all things noble and beautiful."

At one point, Jenny presented Mrs. Kugelmann with a notebook in which she had written a "confession," a popular parlor game at the time, in reply to a list of personal questions. Here are a few extracts:

The quality that I appreciate most in general: humanity.

My dislikes: nobles, priests, military officers.

My favorite activity: reading.

The historical figures I find the most odious: Bonaparte and his nephew.

My favorite poet: Shakespeare.

My favorite writer: Cervantes.

My favorite color: red.

My maxim: "To yourself be true."

My slogan: "All for one and one for all."

A militant of the Spanish section of the International Workingmen's Association (IWA), Anselmo Lorenzo, who met Jenny in 1871, spoke of her in his memoirs (written in the 1920s) as a "memorably beautiful young woman, bright and cheerful, a personification of youth and goodwill." And in another recollection, he wrote that she was "learned and fully conversant in the finer points as she demonstrated when discussing my presentation of Don Quixote, offering a host of considerations I had never heard anyone suggest."

A famous photo depicts her at an early age, posing with Marx, her hand tenderly placed on his shoulder. Her father usually called her Jennychen, but at times used "the Emperor of China" or just "Emperor," no doubt in reference to her Romanesque and youthful reading habits.

In 1872, she married the Communard Charles Longuet, exiled in London, and had six children with him, five boys and one girl. She died in Argenteuil, France in 1883. Her best-known son, Jean Longuet, became an important socialist leader in France.

But what was so special about the year 1871? We received the mysterious Blue Notebook, which is what we decided to call it, a few days later. After a first examination, we found that the pages had yellowed, and some were a bit damaged, but the writing was well preserved. However, it was very difficult to make out.

The entries were first written in German and then French and then English with some French interspersed and vice versa. We called a German comrade, Arno Münster, who was well acquainted with Gothic cursive, and we went to work. It was not an easy task. It took us a long time to decipher the young Jenny's compact hieroglyphs.

From what we managed to read on the first pages, we were perplexed, then astonished. How was it possible? The Blue Notebook revealed a fabulous secret. Jennychen's journal was nothing more and nothing less than a report in miniature of the clandestine visit she made with her father to the Paris Commune, right in the heart of the capital, between April 4 and April 20, 1871.

In the notebook we held, she recounted in detail the secret trip to France with her illustrious father, meetings with several of the Communards—Léo Frankel, Louise Michel, Eugène Varlin, Charles Longuet, Elisabeth Dmitrieff—and intense discussions between Karl and his friends in Paris. Marx's oldest daughter did not confine herself to accompanying her father, pursuing her own interests; she was the one who organized the meeting between her father and Louise Michel. Several pages are, for obvious reasons, dedicated to Charles Longuet. A careful observer, she not only recorded the different sides of the arguments, but also the people, their appearances, their manner of dress, their character, and their attitudes. Her writing is direct, immediate, and without literary, esthetic, or philosophical digressions. She succeeds in capturing the stamp of their socialist and international convictions.

Jenny described her father's activities during their clandestine sojourn with admiration and tenderness, but also with a certain distance and even a kind of irony. Her social and political commitment is evident, yet she is just as interested in the human aspect, in the various sensitivities and sensibilities she finds during their encounters, as she is in the theoretical arguments developed by her father. In fact, while her opinions did not always coincide with those of her father, she carefully reported her father's remarks, his commentaries on events, and his exchanges with the Communards.

Most of the time, she refers to her father as "Moor," his preferred nickname since his studies in Berlin owing to his dark complexion, beard, and jet-black hair, as well as taking inspiration from his Jewish heritage. But just as often she referred to him simply as Father, and when she addressed him directly, Papa.

Jenny shows us a Marx eager to understand this new experience, intensely interested to learn along with the Commune and what it had to teach. Of course, he did not hesitate to offer proposals when he judged it necessary—for example, to confiscate the Bank of France's deposits or to launch a military offensive against Versailles—even when his interlocutors were clearly unconvinced. (He managed only to convince Louise Michel that these proposals were worth considering.)

The Blue Notebook was completed on April 20. Their visit came to an end when Versaillese snitches began spreading rumors about a "Red Prussian" being the secret leader of the Commune. In order to put an end to these damaging insinuations, both Karl and his French colleagues were convinced it was best for father and daughter to return to London.

We do not know if Karl, or later, Charles Longuet, was aware of her diary. If they were, they decided it was best to keep the secret to themselves, probably concerned not to contribute to the reactionary legend that made Marx into the "clandestine conductor" of the revolution. This is, no doubt, the reason Jenny herself preferred to keep it buried at the bottom of a trunk.

We were literally stupefied by the sweep of this discovery. It seemed absolutely incredible that such a visit had gone unknown, or at least unmentioned, by the witnesses. How could it have not been recorded in any other historical document? How could the most gifted historians of the Commune and the best of Marx's biographers have remained ignorant of it? Clearly, Karl and Jenny's Parisian adventure was a secret, but was this enough to explain the silence? Was the Blue Notebook the genuine record of a real visit or the product of a young woman's imagination? As Jenny Marx-Longuet never wrote a work of fiction, we were obliged to take the first hypothesis seriously. It is up to the reader to judge. At any rate, we told ourselves we had to do whatever was necessary to publish this unknown work, even if it remained in many ways mysterious, paradoxical, and inexplicable.

* * *

Once we finished deciphering the work, we were ready to meet with Pierre Longuet to describe the contents of the Blue Notebook and to ask his permission to publish it. We met in the same café where he had first mentioned it to us.

"Pierre, you are going to be shocked, but the Blue Notebook tells the story of a secret trip by Jenny and Karl to Paris during the Commune!"

"That's impossible," Pierre replied incredulously. "Where did you come up with that?"

"We can't explain it, but that's what your great-great-grandmother wrote…"

We then read him some passages from the document and he had to admit that we were not exaggerating. Pierre was just as perplexed as we had been, but at the same time fascinated by the discovery.

"Pierre, would you agree to publish the Blue Notebook?"

"I don't know…Jenny wanted to keep her secret."

"But it's been more than a century. And no one today will accuse Marx of being the clandestine leader of the Commune!"

"I might be accused of having written the notebook myself," worried Pierre. "Of having created a forgery."

"Pierre," we replied," no one can suspect you of writing in Gothic German cursive."

Our friend eventually gave his permission to publish the precious document.

So here it is. In the following pages, we give you the English translation of the French translation of the Blue Notebook. We have had to leave in the original languages a few words that could not be translated. We added the chapter titles ourselves, which were not in the original and which are intended to assist the reader. We have also added, here and there, some explanatory notes. By a happy coincidence, this publication coincides with the 150th anniversary of the Paris Commune. Obviously, the history of that event remains replete with surprises and discoveries for all and this will, no doubt, be true in the decades to come.

Olivier Besancenot
Michael Löwy

1

THE CLANDESTINE VOYAGE

HOW JENNY CONVINCED HER
FATHER TO VISIT PARIS

March 20, 1871

Moor returned from his walk filled with joy. He shook the latest edition of *The Times of London* before our eyes as we looked on in wonder. The official organ of the English bourgeoisie featured a five-column headline shouting, "Red Terrorists Seize Power in Paris."[1] It was the proclamation of the Central Committee of the Commune. I never saw Father so excited.

"The proletariat has taken power! It's the beginning of the social revolution in France, perhaps all of Europe. . . . The Gallic rooster is singing! This is better than 1848, this time they won't corner us like they did in June that year. This time the Reds have the cannons of the National Guard."

A memorable day indeed. We spent two hours picking through the news and trying to comprehend the facts behind the dense fog of the reactionary press. By all accounts, something new and unexpected was underway in Paris, that city of such glorious revolutionary traditions. Over the following days, more and more encouraging information arrived in London. Many of

---

1 Editors' note: "Terrorists" in 1871 did not refer to terrorist attacks, but to the Great Terror of the French Revolution.

our comrades from the International Workingmen's Association (IWA) were elected on March 26, including Léo Frankel and Eugène Varlin.

Some days later, the Commune was proclaimed. Among its first decrees were the abolition of the draft and the standing army!

At that moment, I had an idea.

"Father, why don't we pay a visit to our French comrades? Why don't we go see the city that has built this extraordinary Commune? Paris awaits!"

Moor was hesitant at first.

"Do you think, Jennychen, a German would get a warm welcome?"

"But, Papa, look! They are internationalists, your friend Léo Frankel, isn't he a Hungarian Jew who was raised in Germany? Yet he was elected to the leadership of the National Guard and now to the Commune itself, right?"

"So he was. But there's another, more serious problem. If my presence in Paris became known, Thiers[2] and his clique of rat journalists will quickly accuse the leaders of the Commune of being manipulated by a 'Red Prussian,' a foreign conspirator."

"To be sure, Father," I replied, "It's a problem, but it can be gotten around by keeping our visit a secret. Only our closest friends will know about you being in Paris. It will be necessary to observe the strictest security."

Moor hesitated once again. Mama was none too enthusiastic about my proposition. She found the plan very dangerous and

---

2   Translator's note: Adolphe Thiers was a liberal French politician who rode the waves of French politics for decades. Following Napoleon III's defeat in the Franco-Prussian War, he was elected chief of the new Republican government. A determined opponent of the Commune, Thiers ordered the army to invade Paris in late May 1871.

tried to dissuade us from planning our adventure. Yet Father was more and more taken with the idea of experiencing this unique event in person. Finally, after thinking it over for a few days and becoming increasingly fascinated by the news from the French capital, he made up his mind.

"*D'accord*, Jennychen! I am going to write to Léo to ask what he thinks about our trip. If he agrees, we go. However, the visit must remain truly secret, otherwise, we risk hurting our friends."

The most urgent task was contacting Léo Frankel to get his opinion. Thanks to John Welson, an English journalist sympathetic to the IWA who was sent to cover the Paris events, Father was able to pass a letter to Frankel. Léo responded through the same friend who, as it turned out, made frequent trips between London and Paris. He was delighted by the idea and insisted that Karl come to Paris as soon as possible.

After receiving this message, Moor's hesitancy disappeared; now he had to go. I was in charge of purchasing the tickets after which he sent word to Léo saying we are coming on board a ship arriving in Calais on April 4 at about 2 p.m. In reply, our friend informed us that a young comrade would wait for us at the port to bring us by coach to Paris.

So as to not be recognized, Moor had, at all costs, to change his appearance. After much persuasion, I managed to convince him to dye his hair and trim his beard. At first, he was extremely unhappy with the transformations, but, little by little, he became accustomed to them, even if he continued to grumble about this impertinent obligation.

Mama was shocked upon seeing his metamorphosis and made him solemnly swear that, upon returning home, his appearance would revert to normal.

There remained the thorny problem of getting through customs. An English tailor, John Richardson, who was a friend of Friedrich Engels and a sympathizer of the IWA, and his daughter Sarah helped us in this respect by generously loaning us their passports. They simply claimed later on to have lost them. It is true that Father spoke Shakespeare's language with a slight German accent, but these were subtleties the French border agents were not likely to perceive. My English, by contrast, was impeccable with a typical London accent. In case we were interrogated at the border, we would explain our journey by saying that we needed to buy French fabric for our clothing shop.

Mama packed our bags with spring clothes and some wool (in case the weather turned cold) in expectation of our trip lasting a few weeks, although we had not yet decided on the length of our stay. Father badly wanted to bring a copy of *Capital*, but I convinced him to drop the idea.

"Papa, it's too dangerous. Imagine what could happen if it was discovered by the customs agents. For that matter, who would read it? Frankel already has a copy which you gave him during his last trip to London and the French Communards don't read German!"

Conceding the point, Karl grabbed a copy of Balzac's *Illusions Perdues*, which he intended to reread. Teasing him, I objected to his choice.

"Since when do you read monarchist authors, supporters of the Legitimist Bourbon dynasty?"

"*C'est vrai*," Father replied. "Balzac was a Legitimist. But who better than he to demonstrate the corrupting power of money? I have learned more from him about bourgeois society than from all the economists, statisticians, and theologians combined."

Of course, we agreed. Moor had brought us up in the church of the Romantic writers: Balzac, Dickens, the Brontë sisters, Mrs. Gatskel, all of whom piteously criticized the mores of the bourgeoisie.

April 4, 1871

Mama and Eleanor accompanied us to Dover where we waited for our ship. My sister was a little jealous as she would have liked to go herself. But Karl judged, not without reason, that a larger family delegation might prove difficult for our French hosts to handle. Standing on the platform, Mama pulled me aside. "Watch over your father, Jennychen. Don't let him take any unnecessary risks." "You can count on me, Mama."

This reversal of the usual familial roles amused me greatly. But in the end, she was not wrong to caution me as this trip might prove risky for Moor. In fact, even crossing the Channel had its share of incidents. The majority of the passengers were bourgeois, merchants and factory owners, who never stopped railing against the "Red" Parisians, those criminals, those savages, whose senseless actions were doing great damage to their bottom lines. One in particular declared, hand over his heart, that the French scoundrels ought to be shot. Father had difficulty containing himself, but he knew well that he had to bear the mob in silence. He turned to me and murmured, *"Verfluchte Spiessbürger."*[3] The nauseating hatreds of that class of persons only confirmed his high opinion of the Commune as an authentic expression of the insurgent proletariat.

---

3   Editors' note: A difficult to translate German term meaning "damned bourgeois Philistines."

Upon arriving in Calais, we had to pass through the customs police inspection checkpoint. Moor got through without delay, but I was subjected to an exasperating search! After rummaging through my suitcase, the only object worthy of their attention was a copy of Charles Dickens's *Hard Times*, which I had planned to reread during my Parisian sojourn. Luckily, the police didn't realize it was a dangerous, anti-bourgeois polemic! I was then subjected to a humiliating search of my clothing and, to top it all off, a long interrogation by Monsieur State Prosecutor, the (Bonapartist) Baron Desgarre.

"Miss Richardson, what are your connections with the International Workingmen's Association?"

"Monsieur, I am just a modest dressmaker, I don't know what you're talking about."

"Miss Richardson, what are your connections to the Red Parisians?"

"Monsieur, I have only come to France to purchase some fashionable fabrics."

"Miss Richardson, if you refuse to cooperate, I will be obliged to place you under arrest."

Faced with obstinate silence and the ineffectiveness of his threats, the Baron, this bloody bastard,[4] finally let me leave. Why were they so concerned with me instead of my illustrious father? I have no idea why I was extended such an honor! As they had not discovered my true identity, it is possible my close questioning had to do with young Sarah (that is, the real Sarah Richardson). Perhaps she was active in the IWA with her father and this had drawn the French spies' attention.

---

4   Editors' note: Although this section was originally written in German, Jenny used the English phrase to describe Desgarre.

Moor waited outside, worried and confused. His protests to the officials were ignored. He was relieved to see me emerge and indignant when he learned of my run-in with the cops. He kissed me, obviously very proud.

"I congratulate you, Jennychen, for your courage and your composure in the face of those maniacs."

"Thanks, Papa. Fortunately, they didn't stumble across you. Apparently, they believe I am the more dangerous of the two of us!"

We left as soon as possible, before the sinister Baron Desgarre changed his mind.

Thankfully, the young Jean-François, a goldsmith apprentice who worked with Léo Frankel and had earned his deepest confidence, came looking for us. He drove an old carriage, pulled by two horses who were long in the teeth themselves, but this modest buggy was just the thing to bring us to Paris without attracting undue attention. It was our first contact with a proletarian insurgent. Bright and amiable, Jean-François related the latest of the Commune's military feats with enthusiasm.

"On April 2, we decreed the separation of church and state. At last! And we have indicted Thiers's traitorous government. But the big news from yesterday, April 3, is that we launched an offensive against Versailles."

Moor was thrilled.

"That's outstanding! It's the right course of action to take to win: the best defense is the attack!"

After five or six hours of traveling, the young apprentice delivered us, safe and sound, to Léo's house.

2

LÉO FRANKEL'S HOME

We arrived in Paris at 8 p.m., very tired. Léo Frankel lived in a small house with a garden in La Butte-aux-Cailles. He greeted us warmly, each of his gestures revealing the joy this unexpected visit had brought him.

"Welcome to Paris, my dear Karl and Jenny. Karl, how funny you look! I almost didn't recognize you."

"Blame her," Moor replied, slightly embarrassed. "Jenny made me do it as a security measure."

"My friends, I have two guest rooms and it would give me great pleasure to place them at your disposal. You will be comfortable there and my home is one of the reddest in Paris!"

Father was obviously happy to be staying at his friend's home.

"Thank you, dear Léo, we accept your generous offer. Your home will be our headquarters in Paris."[1]

I playfully teased our friend Frankel, reminding him that he had promised to come to London to teach me how to make jewelry, but he had not kept his word. He eagerly promised to

---

1   Editors' note: In his correspondence, Marx addressed his friends by their last names, "dear Kugelmann," "dear Leibknicht." One of the rare exceptions was Engels, "dear Fred." However, in the Blue Notebooks, Jenny quotes him addressing his friends by their first names. One possible explanation is the more informal nature of spoken exchanges in place of written correspondence.

take me to his workshop, which Jean-François was running in his absence, when he had a little time.

Before he was elected to the Commune by the 13th arron-dissement,[2] Léo had worked as a goldsmith and jeweler and earned a decent living. He was a short man, with a somewhat dark complexion, very dark hair and a short beard of the same color. He dressed simply, but with a certain elegance. His face bore a resemblance to the (broadly speaking) "Central European Jewish" family. His political opponents said he was ugly, but I find this judgment unfair. He spoke fluent German and French, but always with a delicious Hungarian accent. He had met Moor during a stay in London in 1869 and, after devouring the *Communist Manifesto* and a few other political writings by Father and Engels—and perhaps even one or two chapters of *Capital*—had become a convinced partisan of Karl and Friedrich's version of communism.[3] In fact, Léo and Moor became friends, and after he returned to Paris, the two kept up a correspondence. Frankel quickly became one of the main organizers of the French section of the International Workingmen's Association.

In April 1870, he was arrested by the Second Empire's police, along with other IWA activists. Father received updates about his trial and kept us informed. We were impressed by Frankel's courageous speech before his Bonapartist judges, who accused him of "conspiracy:" "We do not hide our objectives. The aim of the International Association is not to raise workers' wages, but to abolish wage labor, which is nothing but disguised slavery."

2   Translator's note: Arrondissement translates roughly to "ward," "district," or "borough" in English.

3   Editors' note: Today, one would say that Frankel was a Marxist, but the term did not exist in 1871.

Imprisoned for a few months, he resumed his activities as an "international" activist as soon as he was released from prison. A member of the National Guard, he was elected on March 26, 1871, as a delegate to the Commune by the 13th arrondissement. He was quite a character, this small Hungarian jeweler...

The next day, April 5, Frankel requested a half-day off from the Commune's Finance Committee to which he had been elected in March and spent some time in dialogue with Moor. Their conversation took place in German, peppered with a few French words. I jotted down their exchanges.

Léo was very proud to report to Moor that the Council had just validated his election to the Commune based on the following argument: "Considering that the flag of the Commune is that of the Universal Republic, foreigners may occupy an elected seat in that body." In his eyes, the Commune had thus reconnected with the noble tradition of the French Revolution, which granted Anacharsis Cloots French citizenship. Cloots had left his native Prussia to come to Paris, a city which, thanks to the Revolution, became "the capital of the world."

Father congratulated him on this achievement, adding, however, with a pinch of irony, "Hopefully you won't end up like Cloots, guillotined by the revolutionaries."

Léo had no such fears.

"That's not likely to happen, dear friend," he explained. "Our Commune has broken with these barbaric practices. As you must have read in my letter at the end of March, I am convinced of the historical importance of what is happening in Paris. If we succeed in radically transforming the social system, the revolution of March 18 will be the most effective of those to have yet taken place."

Moor fully shared this view. For him, the Paris Commune was an unprecedented event: for the first time in history, the proletariat had seized power. Yet, he wanted to know what his friend thought the first steps ought to be in order to approach this radical transformation. As Léo explained to him, not all the members of the Commune were vehement collectivists—for instance, there were Jacobins, Freemasons, moderate Proudhonists, and so on.

Léo felt it was necessary to proceed with caution. Waving the red rag of communism was not the point. It was imperative to find consensus proposals, "common sense" initiatives that could be accepted by any and all.

Father did not disagree with this prudent attitude; he asked Léo for some examples of such initiatives.

Frankel was convinced that a truly socialist measure, and one widely acceptable to his friends, would be the abolition of night-shift work by bakery workers. Their working and living conditions were inhumane, without rest, without family life. And he was determined to fight for this cause.[4]

Moor agreed that this was an important proposition. But he wondered why it should be considered a "socialist" measure, since it did not affect the relations of production.

According to Léo, this measure demonstrated to everyone that only socialism could put an end to the glaring social injustices of bourgeois society.

---

4   On April 20, after the announcement of the decree abolishing bakery night-shift work, Frankel wrote that this was, effectively, "the only genuine socialist decree propagated by the Commune to that date."

Moor sounded less than convinced by this argument, but he didn't want to quarrel with Léo. He preferred to suggest a more radical path.

"Of course," he conceded to Léo. "But shouldn't we also propose initiatives that call into question the private ownership of the means of production?"

"No doubt, dear Karl. I have an idea that just might work. As you may know, many workshops were abandoned by their owners, who fled Paris with the rest of the Versaillese. Should we simply let them rot? Should their workers be condemned to unemployment? I will therefore propose, quite simply, that these abandoned workshops be operated by a cooperative association of the workers who were employed there before the bosses left town."

"Excellent idea, Léo!" exclaimed Moor. "But do you think this measure, in fact, a step in the direction of communism, will be accepted by the majority of the Commune?"

"I think so. We will see!"

Just then, I joined in the conversation.

"Léo, don't you think we should nudge the Commune in the right direction by urging the workers to take the initiative themselves?"

Léo couldn't have agreed more! He described how, in quite a few workshops abandoned by their bosses, the workers had already organized themselves to take charge of their own affairs. In his opinion, this pressure from below would undoubtedly help advance our cause within the ranks of the Commune.

As time ticked by, we were starting to get hungry. Léo was single and did all the cooking himself. He made us an excellent Hungarian goulash, which Moor liked very much. With the exception of the meat, most of the ingredients came from his vegetable and herb garden. As Léo had been very busy since March 18, the garden had been somewhat neglected and needed work, so the three of us got down to pruning. As we pulled up weeds, the conversation continued, but as I was busy cleaning the corner where the tomatoes were growing, I was unable to take any notes.

Léo had collected a large amount of documentation on the events since March 18 for Karl, including decrees issued by the Commune, Council meeting minutes, and copies of newspapers such as *Le Père Duchesne* or *Le Moniteur* (a Versaillese publication).

We spent the next two days in the Butte-aux-Cailles cottage, studying this material and trying to understand the dynamics of these astonishing events. Father took notes, scattering exclamation points or question marks here and there.

On April 8, Léo returned home early from his job at the Finance Commission where he found Moor waiting impatiently for him. He wanted to know about the Commune's financial situation from his friend.

Frankel was a little embarrassed and had to admit it was none too good. The revolutionaries found the municipal coffers almost empty with just enough to pay for the most urgent expenses, some essential services, officials' salaries, and the National Guard's upkeep.

Moor was bewildered.

"Come on, Léo, there's plenty of money in the coffers of the Banque de France! You're not going to leave that in Versailles's pockets, are you? What are you waiting for? You must get your hands on this war chest! If you control the Banque de France, the Versaillese will be ruined."

"Well, I agree with you, Karl, but I'm not sure my comrades in the Finance Committee will. I'll raise it with them anyway."

The next day, when Léo got home in the late afternoon, he looked unhappy. Seeing his face and the way he walked was enough for us to realize that he had failed. He described the outcome of the Commission's meeting to Moor.

"As I expected, my dear friend, my proposal—in fact, it was yours—did not pass. It seems that my companions retain great respect for this venerable institution. Above all, they don't want to be accused of being thieves, people getting rich off public funds. For them, it is a question of principle, a moral question. They fear that the Commune's honorable reputation will be tarnished forever if they touch the Banque de France. The idea of getting their hands dirty with this money is unbearable to them. Blanquists, Jacobins, and Proudhonists, who are often in conflict over different subjects, seem to have found astonishing unanimity on this subject."

"That's really a shame," replied Father. "You are depriving yourself of a trump card in a ruthless class war. In the end, the money in the Banque de France belongs to the people, and you are the people, the Commune! If I could just go to the Finance Committee personally to explain..."

Frankel interrupted him to point out that such a move would immediately reveal his presence in Paris. It was too dangerous, both for him and for the Communards. Besides, he didn't think Moor would have any more luck than he had in convincing this noble Finance Committee, whose loathing of money seemed to be a guiding principle, to change course.

I refrained from participating in this exchange. Basically, I agreed with Father, but I also understood the Committee's ethical concerns.

A few days later, on April 9, we were surprised during breakfast by young Jean-François, who, all out of breath from running all the way to Léo's house, brought us joyful news.

"Have you heard the latest?" he asked. "There's going to be a big celebration of the Commune where we are going to burn the guillotine! It's a historic day!"

We weren't going to miss this, no matter what! So, pushing all other things aside, we rushed over to la Place Voltaire in front of the 11th arrondissement's town hall, where a large crowd was already waiting, gathered around the red flag. We saw National Guard detachments and many workers, including men but in the majority women. As agreed by those responsible for the Commune's justice system, the 137th battalion of the National Guard went looking for two guillotines located in the Roquette prison. The two deadly machines were brought in a cart pulled by two horses and thrown onto a bonfire to shouts of "Vive la Commune!" And "Burn the guillotine!" It was a real popular celebration, joyful and enthusiastic, all taking place under the astounded gaze of Voltaire's statue.

A couple stood beside us tenderly embracing, their eyes riveted on the flames. A National Guardsman, probably an acquaintance, turned to them and exclaimed, "Soon we'll be making a bonfire with their Palace of Versailles!" Presently, a young woman stood out from the crowd. She was dressed in a white shirt and raised her fist, shouting "The Commune or death!" I thought I recognized Elisabeth Dmitrieff, but we were a bit too far away to be able to identify her for certain. Her words were quickly echoed by the National Guard surrounding her. Planks of wood dragged from all around were thrown onto the pyre to fuel the fire, while thick smoke rose to the sky.

Father observed the whole scene, amazed and very happy. Not since 1848 had he seen anything like it. This plebian crowd was not, however, steeped in pacifist illusions. As the flames consumed the hated guillotines, a song arose, emerging from the crowd's bosom, an old revolutionary song from 1793, updated just a little:

> *Monsieur Thiers had promised,*
> *Monsieur Thiers had promised.*
> *To have all of Paris slaughtered,*
> *to have all of Paris slaughtered.*
> *But his attack failed, thanks to our gunners.*
> *Let's dance the Carmagnole, long live the sound, long live the sound*
> *Let's dance the Carmagnole, long live the sound of the cannon!*
>
> *What does a republican demand?*
> *What does a republican embrace?*
> *The equality of the human race,*
> *the equality of the human race.*
> *The rich no longer stand above! The poor not kneeling on the ground!*
> *Let's dance the Carmagnole, long live the sound, long live the sound*
> *Let's dance the Carmagnole, long live the sound of the cannon!*
>
> *Ah, it'll be fine, it'll be fine, Monsieur Thiers up the street light.*
> *Ah, it'll be fine, it'll be fine, Monsieur Thiers we'll hang him high.*

And there you have it. The multitude began to dance the Saint Carmagnole, men and women, old and young, national guardsmen and students, workers and artisans, in a huge procession, singing at the top of their lungs. A whole hour passed before the fire died down and the machines invented by Dr. Guillotin were reduced to ashes. Only then, the crowd began to gradually disperse.

Back at Léo's place, we shared our impressions of the festival. Léo was delighted by the song, which in his eyes was a distillation of socialism: egalitarianism, class struggle, and internationalism ("the human race"), although he did not forget the cannons, just as indispensable a weapon for the proletariat in 1871 as they had been in 1793. Moor was also moved; this was a formidable revolution in his eyes. Of course, the revolution's reference point was the Commune of 1793–94, the glorious tradition of the Sans-Culottes and the Jacobins. But it refused to simply imitate the past. It was inventing something new: a revolution without terror, without the guillotine. The revolution had not forgotten that this machine sacrificed not only Monsieur and Madame Capet,[5] but innumerable revolutionaries: Jacques Hebert and Pierre Gaspard Chaumette (the leaders of the 1793 Commune), Jacques Roux (a radical Catholic priest and precursor of communism), and, finally, Robespierre and Saint-Just themselves.

I couldn't help but add, "Yes, and Olympe de Gouges who pioneered women's rights!"

"Yes, Jennychen, her as well," added Moor. "But the Commune has broken with this past. In the sublime enthusiasm of its historic initiative, the workers' revolution in Paris has made a point of ensuring the proletarians keep their hands clean from the crimes that so often besmirch revolutions, and even more so counter-revolutions by the ruling classes."

---

5   Translator's note: Capet was the surname of Louis XVI and Marie Antoinette.

After dinner we began to consider our next steps. Moor wanted, above all, to meet his internationalist friends: Eugène Varlin, his great ally at the International's Congresses, and Elisabeth Dmitrieff, his young emissary in Paris.

Léo agreed these were good choices. Varlin was his closest comrade in the Council, and he greatly admired Dmitrieff, an extremely brave and energetic girl.[6]

Father wondered if there was anyone else to visit. That's when I spoke up.

"Moor, you forgot my very dear friend Charles Longuet. And you absolutely must meet Louise Michel. From what I've been told, she is an extraordinary character, a revolutionary who is not afraid of anything. I think you will like her."

"All right, Jenny," he acquiesced, "we will go see your Charles Longuet and your Louise Michel."

---

6   Editors' Note: Léo Frankel could not have foreseen that it was Elisabeth Dmitrieff who would save him from death during the Bloody Week. On May 25, Léo and Elisabeth were the last defenders of the barricade of Faubourg Saint-Antoine. Frankel was injured but Elisabeth helped him escape from the Versaillese.

3

CHARLES LONGUET,
THE RED DON QUIXOTE

Toward the end of our first week in Paris, I was starting to get impatient. I wanted to see Charles Longuet again, and I asked Father to schedule this visit as soon as possible.

As always, Father could not deny me anything.

"We'll see him soon, Jennychen. I'm going to ask Léo to make an appointment with him. I like our friend Longuet well enough. He is a bit talkative, but he is a good lad and a great speaker. I've heard him at an IWA Conference before, his speeches sparkle with verve and originality, full of fire and life, and his resounding voice makes the windows shake. With his great stature, upright and sharp, with those enormous arms and interminable legs, he reminds me of the noble Man of La Mancha. He's a kind of red Don Quixote. It's too bad he's remained Proudhonist!"

"Well, Father, I admire his high forehead, his thick black hair, and his big smile. He is a brave fellow, ready to fight for his ideas, to give his life for the cause of justice. Like you, he hates anyone who is lukewarm, 'neutral,' cowardly, anyone who will not take their place on the battlefield of social classes. How many times has he been imprisoned for his rebellious activity? He's always ready to stand up against Napoleon III."

"Of course, he has many good qualities. But, Jennychen, he's been chasing you for six years, since 1865! When are you going to make up your mind?"

"Patience, Father. At the moment, he has other things to worry about."

"No doubt you're right, Jennychen. So many cats, so many colors! You probably have a lot to say to each other between his post as a delegate to the Commune and more, shall we say, personal matters. And while you two catch up, I will take the opportunity to consult the *Journal Officiel de la Commune de Paris*. It contains the Commune's decrees, reports on the debates within the Commune's council, and brief reports about life in Paris. I will take some notes on this material for my report on the Commune for the IWA."

Two days later, Jean-François took us in the carriage to meet with Longuet. The weather was fine, the chestnut trees were in bloom, and the fresh Parisian spring air gave us strength. Along the way our young friend told us the latest news. The day before, he had participated in a meeting of the Club of Notre-Dame-des-Champs, which met regularly in the Church of the same name. Six thousand participants had approved, unanimously, the reduction of rents to less than 500 francs for all tenants! Their demand was sent to the Commune.

In just a few minutes, we were at 39 Quai Voltaire in front of the offices of the *Journal Officiel*, a beautiful classical-style building on the banks of the Seine. Unlike the Hôtel de Ville,[1] there was no checkpoint at the entrance and you could enter just as you pleased. The printing press was located on the ground floor and typesetters bustled all around with lead type, while workers

---

1   Translator's note: Town Hall.

cleaned the press and piles of newspapers were stacked up on the floor, making passage through the room a delicate operation. We took the stairs, which were a little steep, but luckily not cluttered with newspapers. On the first floor, the few reporters scribbling articles for the next day's edition ignored our presence.

Finally, on the second floor, we found our dear Charles waiting for us. His office was austere, without unnecessary décor. Mounted on the wall, an angular stain marked the empty spot where a portrait of Napoleon III had undoubtedly been mounted. His worktable, a handsome piece of First Empire–style ebony furniture, was littered with papers, newspaper clippings, and handwritten notes. Standing in the middle of the living room, he looked even taller, even thinner, than when we last met in London. His dark eyes were sharp and piercing, but also timid and gentle. I was delighted to see him again, and my feelings were hard to hide. With a wave of his long, gaunt arm, he invited us to sit in two comfortable enough chairs a short distance from his table, where he then took his place.

Like our other interlocutors, he was surprised by the effectiveness of Moor's disguise, but his gaze immediately turned to me with a great intensity.

"Welcome, dear Marx and dear Jenny! I am very happy you've come to visit!"

"And we," replied Moor, "are extremely happy to be in Paris, the insurgent capital of Europe, the first great proletarian city of modern history. You are the heirs to two thousand years of class struggles, from Spartacus's slave revolt right up until today."

"I hope we will do better than our ancestors," he replied, smiling. "After all, they were slaughtered by the Roman Legions! We will know how to defend ourselves."

"I share your hope, that goes without saying. But don't you believe, as Commander of the 248th Battalion of the National Guard, that the best defense would be an attack? What do you think of the possibility of an offensive against Versailles?"

Charles thought for a few moments. Obviously the answer was not straightforward. But when he finally offered us his opinion, it was rather negative.

"Frankly speaking, I do not believe it is possible. We could have, perhaps, closed the gates of Paris on March 18 to prevent the government from leaving for Versailles. But an attack outside Paris would be doomed to failure. Our National Guard is a popular army, not prepared to fight traditional military battles against a professional army. However, it will be able, I firmly believe, to resist any attack on Paris from the outside."

Father did not look convinced, but, not knowing the true state of the forces involved, he refrained from commenting. He took the floor again to address another subject, this one just as delicate: the political composition of the Commune. He wanted to know Charles's opinion as to whether, as Engels believed, the majority was composed of Blanquists with a minority of Proudhonists like Longuet himself.

Charles proudly responded that he admired Blanqui as much as Proudhon. In his opinion, Engels was wrong because the Blanquists were only a small minority. "The Commune's Council is a beautiful mixture, very heterogeneous," he explained. "You can find everyone there, including Jacobins, of course, a few Blanquists, all kinds of collectivists and socialists, and revolutionaries without precise economic doctrines. And in the minority, belonging to the ranks of the IWA, there are mutualists, libertarian communists, revolutionary Proudhonists, and even some supporters of Moor's ideas, such as Léo Frankel. But we also find," he added with a burst of laughter, "some rather bizarre figures among our comrades of the IWA."

Astonished, Father wanted to know who these strange characters were. With a good dose of irony, Charles described a certain Régère de Montmore to him who was, no doubt, an uncompromising revolutionary, an internationalist, but also ... a practicing Catholic, who made his son take his first communion at Saint-Sévérin Church! On the other hand, he had no problem at all with the Commune taking Monseigneur Darboy, the Archbishop of Paris, and a few other priests hostage: "They're political enemies, aren't they?"

The story amused Moor, who was unfamiliar with this typically Parisian kind of political eccentricity.

Longuet added, with a smile, that he was describing this character just to show us the plurality, the extraordinary diversity of the Commune. He recognized that sometimes it could result in quite a cacophony; however, when it came to important questions, the Commune's Council managed to find a common language. For example, all were in agreement, whether mutualists, collectivists, or Jacobins, about turning workshops abandoned by their bosses over to workers' societies.

Each time Father heard about this initiative, he made a point of paying homage to the Commune's foresight, and he explained to Longuet why he considered this decision, foreshadowing the communist society of the future, both courageous and necessary. However, he couldn't refrain from asking Charles a somewhat touchy question.

"Despite your friendship and admiration for Blanqui, with whom you have worked closely, and your interest in my writings, have you not remained, after all, a Proudhonist?"

A little embarrassed by this direct question, Charles explained himself, perhaps a little defensively, but refusing to disguise his views.

"You know, dear friend, one does not change one's beliefs in the same way as one changes the bedsheets. I quite agree with your criticisms of Proudhon's writings up to 1851. The criticism you made in *The Poverty of Philosophy* (1847) of his first economic works, which were still quite imbued with a petite-bourgeois spirit, seem to me to be correct. On the other hand, the Proudhon of 1853 and after—and especially in his book *Of the Political Capacity of the Working Classes* (1865)—was a true anti-authoritarian socialist, and a supporter of the producers' association ... just like you!"

Of course, Moor took this suggestion skeptically. He didn't want to polemicize with his friend, but he couldn't help pointing out how little in common there was between Proudhonian mutualism and his own communist program. Besides, in his eyes, the most essential question lay elsewhere, in the capacity of the Commune, both its leaders and the workers, the National Guard ranks, the artists, and the rest, to act in common, to push this admirable proletarian revolution closer toward the emancipation of labor.

Delighted with Moor's positive conclusion, Charles remained quiet. He had nothing else to add.

Taking advantage of the brief silence, Father, who had not forgotten the reason for his visit, asked Charles for permission to consult the Commune's *Journal Officiel* so he could take some notes for a report he intended to write for IWA.

Charles was happy to oblige. He explained to Moor that this modest journal, which he directed as a delegate of the Commune, was a faithful mirror of the Commune's decisions and debates and invited his friend to follow him to the publication's archive room.

We followed him down a hallway cluttered with piles of newspapers and came to a large room, the walls of which were laden with long, dusty shelves. Charles explained to us that most of them were dedicated to the *Journal Officiel de l'Empire Français* and that only a small shelf was reserved for the Commune's newspaper. Moor took a seat at a table with an inkwell and quills, and fetched some newspapers from the shelf. We left him there to work and returned to the editor's office.

Now it was my turn to talk with Charles about more personal matters.

"Dear Charles, I am so delighted to see you again and you haven't changed a bit, so proud, so devoted to our cause, and, at the same time, so full of sweetness."

"My little Jenny, you can't imagine how much I have missed you these years since we met in London. Seeing you here has filled me with unspeakable happiness."

To lighten the mood, I said, with a smirk, "I hope you haven't fallen in love with Elisabeth Dmitrieff, like Léo and Varlin!"

"I admire our dear Elise very much, but you, Jenny, are the only one who matters to me."

"You asked me to marry you in London."

"Yes, and I still want that. But I had no choice but to return here to fight this nefarious, miserable Bonapartist Empire alongside the Republicans and the IWA. And now, as you see, I cannot abandon my trench, so long as the revolution is threatened from all sides. But I solemnly promise you that, if I live through this extraordinary adventure, I will come to London to marry you. Of course, 'La Commune ou la Mort!' may complicate my desire," he added with a timid smile. "If we do not triumph over the Versaillese, many of us will perish on the barricades, defending our revolution to the last breath."

"I know how courageous and determined you are, and I have no intention of dissuading you from fighting for the Commune. But your life is precious, you must protect it, the International needs you... not to mention our own future together."

We chatted for quite a while longer, but I stopped taking notes...

Eventually, Moor returned from the archive. He was enthusiastic and held in his hand the *Journal Officiel* of March 20, where he had found one of the very first revolutionary proclamations, which he read aloud to us.

"The proletarians of the capital, in the midst of the failings and betrayals of the ruling classes, understood that the time has come for them to save the situation by taking charge of the administration of public affairs."

Father waved his hands as he spoke and, without letting go of the newspaper, assumed the solemn tone he adopted when pronouncing what he considered important statements. For him, the proclamation was a striking example of what makes the Commune great; that is, for the first time in history, we have a government of the working class. Even better, for the first time, after the people's first uprising, they did not disarm themselves and place their power in the hands of the Republican political acrobats from the ruling classes. Instead, by forming the Commune, they seized the revolution's leadership for themselves.

Something in that comment didn't seem to sit right with Charles, and he asked whether Father believed the Commune had simply replaced the domination of the bourgeois class with the despotism of the working class.

"No, dear Longuet," replied Moor. "I think the Paris Commune is a social and democratic republic, whose leaders are no longer haughty and despotic masters of the people, but servants who may be revoked at any time. And the Commune defends the interests of all the popular classes, not only the workers, but also the middle classes, the petty bourgeoisie, and the peasantry. It says it all in your own *Journal Officiel*. Just look at the main initiatives taken so far. Several of them favor the middle classes, for instance, protecting debtors against creditors and suspending the legal proceedings of rent collection, to name just two."

Our red Don Quixote listened attentively. He did not disagree with Moor, but he reminded his interlocutor that the Commune had also authorized repressive measures, for example, the taking of hostages. Charles admitted that this decision made him uncomfortable.

Father understood his scruples, but he tried to convince his friend of the merits of the Commune's decisions. What a paradoxical dialogue; the London guest had fewer doubts than the Communard leader!

"What else could the Commune have done, faced with the Bonapartist thieves' atrocious provocations and Thiers's summary executions of prisoners? It was only proper for the Commune to take several hostages and threaten reprisals; yet these threats have remained a dead letter!" complained Father. "Remember that even when police sergeants were caught with explosives, they were not brought to a court-martial. The Commune refused to dirty its hands with these dogs' blood! Alas, as soon as the Versailles government was convinced that the Commune was too humane to carry out its decree of April 6 to execute three hostages for every National Guard prisoner killed by Theirs, Versailles renewed its killing spree with stepped-up fury."

This last argument seemed to convince Charles.

"You are right. But we have given an example of humanity that contrasts with the bloody crimes of the Versaillese."

"But you must not forget that you are at war," Moor reminded Charles. "It is a real civil war, labor's against those who monopolize the means of production against capital."

Charles agreed, of course. But, speaking of hostages, he shared with us his regret that the Commune had not taken the only hostage that mattered, the one hostage worth ten thousand men, the Banque de France...

Father obviously shared this point of view, but he asked Longuet to explain the reasons for this timidity.

Charles explained to him that C. Beslay, who was appointed by the Commune as delegate to the Banque de France, was convinced that by seizing the central credit institution by force of arms, *manu militari*, the Commune would provoke a general depreciation of French banknotes, which would become as worthless as the assignats currency issued in 1789. Not being an economist, Longuet did not feel in a position to judge and had soon withdrawn from the Finance Committee.

At that moment our conversation was interrupted by a messenger who brought Charles a document. This was a new decree the Commune had just issued, dated April 12, to be published in the *Journal Officiel*.

Charles read it to us, in a voice filled with emotion.

"Decree to demolish the column in Place Vendôme, a monument to barbarism, a symbol of naked force and false glory, an affirmation of militarism, the negation of international law."

Charles had always hated nationalism, to the point that Father had once criticized him for his Proudhonist attitude of denying the actuality of nations. But Charles couldn't hide his joy.

"Wonderful!" he cried. "Our artist friend, Gustave Courbet, has been fighting for this decision for several days. I'm very pleased to see it passed, and we will publish it tomorrow in the *Journal Officel*, pending its application. Nefarious nationalism, this vestige of ancestral savagery, this latest form of primitive anthropophagy, that is what we are demolishing with this column!"[2]

Moor joined Charles in celebrating without reservation; he saw this resolution as a magnificent symbol. The Commune was breaking with the historical and political heritage of Bonapartism. The column, this scarecrow made of bronze from cannons captured from "enemy" armies, embodied everything he hated: the warrior spirit, contempt for other nations, the desire for conquest, the arrogance of the decorated officer caste.

Moor considered the Commune's decision to be a formidable act of revolutionary internationalism, and this provided Charles an opportunity to express his high opinion of my father, despite the few but major differences between them.

---

2 Editors' Note. The demolition of the Colonne Vendôme took place in May after Jenny and her father had already left Paris.

"An internationalism of which you, the great inspirer of the IWA's resolutions, are one of the most eminent representatives in the world! I know that you are an uncompromising supporter of materialism, a historical materialism with which you analyze the misdeeds of the propertied classes. But deep down, you are a generous idealist, your home in London is open, in a spirit of international solidarity, to outlaws from all countries, and from all popular causes. You welcome them without conditions or doctrinal reservations, lavishing the most cordial hospitality on them. You and your daughter embody all the best of that idealized image of the romantic knight of La Mancha."

Father was touched by this friendly tribute as he greatly admired Don Quixote. But he reminded his friend that the Commune was not tilting against windmills. The evil giants against which it struggled really did exist, even if they took the form of a hideous gnome in the infamous Thiers. And to defeat them, he insisted, with a hint of irony, it is not enough to ride an old horse, a valiant Rocinante, spear in hand; instead, it required rifles, machine guns, and cannons!

Longuet immediately assured Moor that the Commune would not fail to use its cannons to face the repugnant Versaillese giants, armed to the teeth, whether they were led by Thiers himself or generals Trochu, Vinoy, or Galliffet.

Hearing this reference to the sinister politicians and generals of Versailles, Father fell silent and began pacing around the study from the window to the door and back. He was worried, explaining to Charles that he feared there was a secret agreement between Thiers and Bismarck. His evidence? Thiers groveled in the Prussian leader's dust in each of his speeches. Nothing separates them now that they have found a common enemy in insurgent Paris. Bismarck, whose troops occupy the fields north of Paris, won't attack the Commune, but he might easily allow the Versaillese troops to pass by unimpeded in order to invade Paris through the northern suburbs. Father was of the opinion that the National Guard should fortify the northern slope of the Buttes Montmartre facing the Prussians.

Charles promised him that he would pass along these wise observations to his friends in the National Guard. "The difficulty comes, however," he added, "from the fact that the Commune had to strengthen its defenses in all four cardinal points, not knowing where the attack will come from."

Moor continued, advising that the enemy always attacks where you least expect them. But it was getting late and it was time to go.

"Thank you for entertaining us, dear Longuet. We don't want to detain you any longer, you have to prepare tomorrow's *Journal Officiel*."

So we took leave of Charles, although after Father left the room, I stayed behind in his arms for just a few more minutes. I prayed to Clotho, Lachesis, and Atropos, the Greek Goddesses of Destiny—the Moirai—that he would live, come what may.

4

ELISABETH DMITRIEFF AND THE WOMEN'S UNION

CAFÉ DES NATIONS, 79 RUE DU TEMPLE

We arrived punctually at the meeting that Léo had organized just for us. It was 7 a.m., barely dawn. Squinting in the dim light, I had to double-check the address I had written down on a piece of paper. No mistake, we were at number 79 Rue du Temple, facing the baroque storefront of the Café des Nations, one of those typically Parisian dives. Moor wasn't going to admit it, but his slow pace gave away his state. He had spent the night coughing and was exhausted. Discreetly, I took the lead to open the door for him, but before my hand even reached the doorknob, the doors squealed loudly, announcing our intrusion. Once inside, we hesitated for a moment before pushing through the thick purple curtains that blocked access to a small circular area that was meant to serve as a vestibule. Elisabeth was waiting for us just behind these makeshift curtains.

Lisa was a young woman from Russia that our family had recently fallen in love with in London and whom Father had assigned a few weeks earlier to follow the course of events in Paris. She was to serve as an observer on behalf of the International Workingmen's Association, but that assignment came to grief upon her arrival, the day after the proclamation of the Commune.

Our Russian Lady, lacking precise directions, had preferred, it seems, to join in the intoxicating whirlwind of the revolution.

Léo informed us that our recently arrived "special correspondent" had been immediately taken up with tasks far more exhilarating than writing detailed reports for the International. Her decision was affected by the none-too-friendly reception the Paris section of the International had offered her where Father's political program had irritated many of the local members. His writings never failed to arouse controversy on the premises of the Place de la Corderie, the International's Paris office. The same could not be said about the commonplace machismo in the Paris office, which did not suffer from any such discord. On this subject, Proudhon's misogynistic conceptions had done lasting damage to the comrades' minds. I could only imagine the mistrust to which Lisa must have been subjected. She was a woman, young, beautiful, intelligent, charismatic, close to Marx, aristocratic, and, to top it all off, Russian. In their eyes, she had a long list of strikes against her.

But Lisa did not let this get her down and she decided to take another path, linking her fate to that of the insurgency. By the time she dropped off her luggage in her modest apartment on Boulevard de Saint-Ouen, she was doing all she could, in her own measure, to ensure the Commune's success. Lisa soon gained a reputation as a daring preacher of the social revolution. Her Russian intonations intrigued her audiences, and she easily captured the attention of crowds that she ended up captivating. She had a disconcerting ability to speak plainly without getting sidetracked, which was rare enough in her generation of rebellious, romantic, and impatient youth, born out of the political struggle against Russian Emperor Alexander II in the 1860s. She

possessed a natural eloquence she had later refined during her exile in Geneva, amidst a diaspora of political refugees from all over
the world. Father liked to say that the French insurgents were
"storming heaven" and Lisa came out of nowhere, blazing across
the sky like a shooting star.

The meeting between the two of them was striking in many
ways. Her name circulated within the capital. A rumor, shroud-
ed in mystery, had even reached the ears of the sinister Adolphe
Thiers, who was, however, unaware that her surname was in reality only a wartime pseudonym, francophied and invented by
Lisa just before crossing the Channel from London under a false
identity. We were not going to visit Lisa Tomanovskaïa in that
Parisian bistro, but Madame Elisabeth Dimitrieff, the recently
promoted president of the Women's Union for the Defense of
Paris and the Care of the Wounded.

Léo had explained to us that this movement had caused a lot
of ink to be spilled right from the start. In less than a week of
existence, we had already lost count of the exploits attributed to
its work. Its founding manifesto, handwritten by Lisa on April
11, was a burning match set to a barrel of powder. She had literally set the hearts of the women of Paris on fire. "Citizens, the
gloves are off. We will either live or die. And if we have neither
rifles nor bayonets, we will dig up the cobblestones to crush the
traitors." Such a call could not go unnoticed, neither among the
ranks of the Communards nor those of the Versaillese, who were
informed each day of the slightest subversive activity thanks to an
army of snitches watching the population. Everyone here feared
these spies.

Thus, Léo had preferred to arrange the meeting for day-
break, in order to escape prying ears and eyes. He assuredly

accomplished his mission as I think it would have been difficult to find a more deserted place than this cabaret. The large main room was filled with empty tables, scattered all around. Our shadows, lit by little kerosene lamps hanging here and there, danced along the walls and grew larger as we stepped between the abandoned chairs. A day-after calm hung in the air, sign of a well-deserved rest after what must have been a boisterous party. Only a few clinking glasses in the background broke the silence at regular intervals. The floor featured light beige tiles adorned with black outlines and traces of a soiled carpet that gave the impression of having been trampled on by an entire garrison. And some none-too-pleasant odors testified to the previous night's carousing. After crossing a courtyard, we finally reached the bar, a large zinc counter being polished meticulously by an imposing woman. Without a word, she raised her chin toward a guard, letting him know that we were expected. Father removed his hat and tried to greet her but was met with an indifferent glance. I was blessed by this sentry, on the contrary, with a broad smile, sisterly and toothless. No doubt, we had just entered one of the many lairs in Parisian neighborhoods where the proletarian women made the rules. I laughed to myself, thinking that Moor had probably never come face to face with the "flesh-and-blood proletariat" he so often praised in his articles in such a way. The women in this bar, "proletarians of the proletarians," had nothing of a sophisticated philosophical abstraction about them. Without a word, we followed the landlady's instructions, stepping over an old mop at the end of its life prostrate on a hardwood floor.

Obviously busy reading the papers, Lisa was sitting at a table. She straightened up and gave us both a warm hug. The silence of our reunion spoke volumes about the emotions that gripped us all. Although her image remained clear in my memory, I was unsettled by the charisma emanating from her. She was so young—barely twenty—and so mature at the same time. Her round chin and slender forehead, untouched by time, evoked adolescence, while her piercing gray-blue gaze betrayed a hardened character, accustomed to life's vagaries. I found her complexion unusually pale, yet she was beaming. The immense accumulated fatigue suggested by her drawn features had not affected her style. Her brown hair was, as usual, wrapped effortlessly up in a bun. Her gestures were always so graceful and delicate. Dressed all in black, in a long, elegant velvet dress, she wore a scarlet scarf cinched around her waist. She looked like a Russian princess in sans-culottes garb. Lisa was looking us over as well, suppressing a slight grin at the sight of Father's outfit. She cleared her felt hat from one of the chairs and invited us to sit down.

"*Dobroe utro,*" she welcomed us in her native tongue. "My dear friends, I have missed you so much! Just a month ago, we were preparing this trip together from your office, Karl, at 1 Modena Villas in London. Yet I feel that years have passed. Everything is going so fast here, I hardly know where to turn. The days are too short to complete the avalanche of tasks the Commune demands of us. Every moment is rich with experience, and consciousness evolves by the hour, uprooting the exploited from the torpor into which the Empire had plunged them for decades. But here I am already starting a speech without having bothered to hear from you! Jenny, I want to commend your powers of persuasion. You alone were able to convince your father to cross the English Channel. And you Karl, your health? You are unrecognizable. A real Parisian."

"My dear Lisa," Moor replied. "Thank you for setting aside a part of your precious time to share with us. You can only imagine the thousand and one questions I wish to ask, but your responsibilities force us to get to the point. But I have to first ask about you. You must be exhausted! These smoky clubs where you hold meetings can't be good for your bronchitis. You have to take care of yourself. Although, from a political point of view, I must admit that the Parisian air becomes you! It is clear that these proud people of the Commune have definitively made you their own."

"You wouldn't believe it, Karl! Just yesterday evening, within these very walls, the general assembly of the Union des Femmes honored me with the title of 'citizen of Paris,' asking the Universal Republic to naturalize me and name me a 'citizen of humanity.' The Commune has attracted thousands of internationalist foreigners, Prussians, Italians, Belgians. And there are other Russians like me such as the writer Piotr Lavrov, an old acquaintance, and the Korvin-Krukovsky sisters, both close to Dostoevsky and whom I had met in St. Petersburg. Poles have also entered the spotlight, generals Dombrowski and Wroblewski are in charge of our military defense. As for the nomination of our friend Léo, a Hungarian, to the post of labor delegate, it still sticks in the throats of the Versaillese who see it as irrefutable proof of the International's omnipotence. Karl, if he got wind of your coming, Thiers would go mad, really *zloy ot yarotsi*! He would have Paris covered with your wanted poster. Take my friendly advice, and I don't mean this as a reproach, when I say *prosta* that you really have to be careful. Things do not bode well, especially since the Versailles 'Pantalons rouges' troops have captured Fort-de-Vanves. At this very moment they are ripping open our defenses when we should have gone out first and marched on Versailles. In the civil war to come, we will have to fight to the death and cross our fingers that the looming confrontation is not so deadly as to stifle the many projects the Commune intends to carry out."

"Lisa, I can't say if you are going to war, but I understand the urgency of the situation," replied Father. "Civil war is Thiers's central aim, this monstrous dwarf who has managed to hold the French bourgeoisie under his spell for nearly half a century by adapting to circumstance and by hedging his bets with each successive regime. He wants to conduct a massacre in Paris as an example because the Commune is a singular experience in the history of the class struggle, the very existence of which represents a threat to the bourgeoisie. I admit I underestimated him at first. Perhaps I was obsessed with the German situation, where material conditions seemed more advanced to me. It just goes to show that the chain of domination can be broken at any moment where you least expect it. Under the reign of Louis Bonaparte, during the Second Empire, the ruling class had found the perfected form of state power capable of countering the popular threat, that is, a national regime dedicated entirely to prosecuting capital's war against the workers. The Commune is the antithesis of the Empire, an inversion of history where labor achieves ascendancy over capital. Léo told us about your common intentions to found federated workshops, in textiles in particular. A plan developed by the Union des Femmes, which could be authorized by his ministry."

"You should know that the Union des Femmes owes a lot to Nathalie Le Mel, who is also a member of the International," said Lisa, praising her comrade. "She is close to Varlin whom I met in Geneva last year. We hit it off right from the start. I think of her as a kind of big sister. Her rebellious Breton character and her staunch pragmatism make her one of the pillars of the Union, and she helps ground us firmly amidst the effervescence of Parisian political life. Remember! Paris is a boiling pot, permanently supplied by an incalculable number of revolutionary clubs and neighborhood committees. The Commune draws its sap up from the roots before it's concentrated at the Hôtel de Ville. In fact, the uprising of the Parisian people has been taking place for several months now. The Commune was officially born on March 18, but it was smoldering deep in the old world's belly long before the siege. By the end of the Second Empire, communalist fires, unbeknownst to one another, were undermining the foundations of the old order. The municipal elections of March 27 represent nothing more or less than the outcome of this slow democratic fertilization, long biding its time. Nathalie became an activist during this long and difficult cycle of political gestation, and she learned to impose her character on fiery and exclusively male forums. She is not only a renowned speaker, she is also an outstanding organizer. Endless discussions about the world after the revolution did not distract her from her immediate objectives. With Varlin's support, she succeeded in setting up a food cooperative in record time as well as gigantic workers' cafeterias called 'la Ménagère' and 'la Marmite,'[1] to prevent the poorest people from succumbing to hunger during the winter. More than eight thousand people have benefited from this mutual aid. When we called for the Union des Femmes, we weren't starting from nothing. We earned legitimacy with the proletarians over time. Our political expectations were all the higher because of this work. Hence the spectacular turnout at our meetings."

Listening to her speak, I realized how much Lisa had changed in such a short time. She conveyed a sense of self-confidence, even authority. However, one could detect in her a carefully suppressed

---

1   Translator's note: "The Housekeeper" and "The Cooking Pot."

fragility, an unspeakable and discreet flaw. Her frenetic and communicative enthusiasm masked dark, almost indifferent expressions. The sacred fire of revolution was burning within her stronger than ever, but a sensitive chord, hidden in a corner of her soul, appeared about to snap at any moment. She no longer seemed to belong to herself, as if the cause forced her to withdraw. I sensed that Moor was anxious and even for worried her. I took it upon myself to renew the thread of our conversation to jolt him out of his thoughts.

"Tell me Lisa, what kind of goals has the Union des Femmes set for itself? Are you caring for the wounded?"

"Yes, but we are not limited to that, far from it. We refuse to be relegated to the rank of assistants to the revolution. Of course, we have many first-aid workers and nursing assistants, whose roles are as vital as they are risky because Theirs intentionally fires on our ambulances under the pretext that we have not ratified current international conventions. As if we could. But we refuse to stand at the Commune's bedside; we aspire to be recognized for what we are in truth, that is, citizens and combatants. We are as courageous as the men."

Lisa was talking to me, but I knew her words were addressed mainly to Father in order to convince him of one of the revolution's particularities, namely, that women were the great instigators. You found them propagating the emancipatory values of the Commune on every street corner in Paris. Be they in unsanitary hovels, posh cafes, workshops, barracks, public meetings, theaters, or on the barricades, no place in the capital escaped them. Their determination exasperated the Versaillese as much as it made them tremble. Especially since they had not waited until March 1871 to open a path. In fact, since the proclamation of the

Republic on September 4, 1870, and during the many insurrectionary days, including when Place de l'Hôtel de Ville had been set ablaze during the siege, women had always taken an active part in the struggle, never deserting the battle lines. Moreover, on the very day of its founding, March 18, the Commune would probably have let its artillery slip into the hands of the Versaillese were it not for the women! Who had sounded the call to arms that morning on Butte-Montmartre to rally the crowd and save our cannons? The vigilance committee of the citizens of the 18th arrondissement chaired by Louise Michel. When the Versaillese carried out their first military attacks in Courbevoie at the beginning of April, it was women who immediately called for a march on Versailles. On April 3, according to Lisa, one thousand women at la Place de la Concorde called for a massive expedition to reinforce the garrisons of Flourens and Duval and deal a fatal blow to the aggressors. They had even tried to cross the fortifications in order to go to their comrades' aid, but the National Guard had prevented them from doing so. And when the Parisian government sitting at the Hôtel de Ville, paralyzed by incessant chatter, was once again reluctant to send all available forces, the Council's promises of action were no longer enough. The women of the Commune grew impatient. They therefore decided to organize themselves. Father was listening to Lisa's story but something seemed to arouse his curiosity.

"Wasn't the Women's Committee of the International sufficient?" he asked.

"Let's just say that the time had come to see the big picture," replied Lisa diplomatically. "And that this idea was not necessarily unanimous within the IWA's Women's Committee with which I had been put in contact with by Benoît Malon, one of leaders of the International whom you know, when I arrived in Paris. We therefore launched a public appeal to women to take up arms. Our motto was clear: 'Live free working or die fighting!' As soon as it appeared in the Commune's *Journal Officiel* Municipality—and the next day in *La Sociale*—our proclamation met with success that exceeded even our own expectations. Our manifesto was pasted on the city walls and groups of women gathered around to read it under the anxious gaze of passers-by in their Sunday best. Some of them, more educated than others, read the proclamation out loud. I can still hear them repeat the words, 'The struggle for the defense of the Commune is the struggle for women's rights!'"

Lisa was so exhilarated that her breathing started to falter at the end of each sentence. Father broke in hoping she would catch her breath.

"Take a breath, Lisa! I hear what you are saying. Your analysis is convincing. Your movement seems to be winning over the hearts of the Parisian proletariat."

"Absolutely. Among the Union's eight thousand members, those from the bourgeoisie or the aristocracy, like me, are in the extreme minority. Our army counts in our ranks many workers, seamstresses, bar maidens, laundresses, clothiers, and shopkeepers as well as those without a profession, including many who are single or widowed. All demand the right to work as well as equal pay, secular education free of charge for boys and girls, and the creation of collective child care centers, but also civic and legal equality, including the right vote. After all, even in the eyes of the men of the Commune, we remain second-class citizens, neither eligible to stand for office nor vote."

Lisa explained to us how often they had had to pound their fists on the table to get each district town hall to provide them with decent premises to set up recruiting offices. There were one or two districts who remained defiant in the face of the Union's demands, but in many places, the Union's offices had enabled women to participate in municipal management. The Union intended to be grafted onto the communal model, adding to the International's effectiveness. The activity of each of the local assemblies was centralized through a permanent district committee, composed of eleven members. Each of them reported on a daily basis to the Parisian central committee where Lisa sat. The latter organized two or three sessions per day, most often in a room at the Marie in the 3rd arrondissement. While explaining all this to us, Lisa was suddenly seized with a nasty cough which she managed to contain gracefully.

"Excuse me," said Lisa, clearing her throat. "The days are busy and sleep has become a scarce commodity. Even more precious than food. But if you only knew how high the stakes were. I feel like here I am living through the real-life manifestation of all the things we discussed in your London parlor. How many hours have we spent considering the socialist potential of traditional Russian peasant communities! I can still see you pacing in front of the fireplace, cigar in hand, the *People's Cause* under your arm, and examining the point of view advocated by our Russian section's newspaper. Do you remember?"

"How could I forget our exchanges!" replied Moor. "You never failed to quote this or that passage from your favorite novelist, Chernyshevsky! I admit that his book *What Is to Be Done?* piqued my curiosity and that, thanks to you, it prompted me to reflect on forms of communitarian organization. But I didn't realize how much his story had captured your imagination and how closely it guided your every step. I see that here in Paris you have managed to slip into the skin of your favorite character, Véra Pavlovna. A wedding of convenience to escape from your social environs; the thirst for the ideal bond and individual freedom; an allergy to any form of authoritarianism; your talents as an "orator," an affectionate title bestowed upon you by your comrades, to whom you do not give orders but only offer counsel. You have definitely adopted your heroine's habits! As for this project of cooperatives run by seamstresses, it will enable the Chernyshevsky novel to come to life. Vera would be proud of you.

"Returning to the main point, your proposal for seamstress workshops, run entirely by the workers, would be a first. These factories of a new type would indeed found new working communities, a Parisian worker cooperative version of the old Russian peasant *artels*. Your workshops would hold the machines and the fabric in common, in place of the land, tools, and livestock pooled by the traditional rural artels. I must admit that the logic of the autonomous peasant communities, the *obscina*, that you described so passionately to me partly overlaps with that of communalist democracy—with the notable difference that the latter is the act of the working class itself, based on its own experience, and thereby poses the questions of collective property in unprecedented ways. The Commune is a concrete attempt to throw off the yoke of capital itself. A prospect dangerous enough to make exploiters around the world tremble. Do you realize, Lisa, the city of light has become, in earnest, home to 'the impossible' communism, a reality very far from utopias? The bells of Notre-Dame are sounding the death knell for capitalism, a vision so terrifying for the bourgeoisie that we must face the danger of them striking out from the depths of their fears. Léo told me that you were concerned about the communal government's inertia with respect to calling for an uprising throughout the province. You're right. The crushing of the Communes of Lyon and Saint-Etienne, and more recently in Marseille and Narbonne, makes us fear the worst if the Paris Commune fails to rally the French peasantry against Versailles. But one thing is certain: this uprising will be a milestone in the history of socialist thought, demonstrating, I hope once and for all, that ideas do not fall from the sky, rather they are revitalized in the face of a practical action."

"I agree with everything you say," smiled Lisa. "This might be a first! Our experiment might still succeed and demonstrate its promises. Yet not everyone shares your enthusiasm for cooperatives. Just think! The military warehouses of Alésia and Denfert are overflowing with stocks of fabrics already paid for, they only need to be requisitioned to begin producing the uniforms needed by the National Guard. The same goes for rifle cartridges and the sandbags our barricades and our fortifications need. Not only are women workers able to manufacture what we lack, but they could produce it, for the first time, under a social regime where the fruits of our labor would no longer be monopolized by a handful of profiteers. On this point too, our call was unequivocal: 'We want to work, but we aim to keep the products of our labor... Without exploiters and without masters.' In each arrondissement, cooperatives could meet the needs of the population, operating autonomously, without cutting themselves off from the links and coordination provided by the Commune's Commission. We might even wager that this kind of federation of free producers will one day bring together the various Communes throughout France. And, ultimately, beyond our borders. However, for the time being, the Commune prefers to continue doing business with the companies with the widest offerings. Even if the wages of workers suffer! Nothing is settled, Karl, far from it. Our ideas make some people at the Hôtel de Ville choke. Some may imitate Robespierre's intonations but their determination does not live up to their words. When it comes to attacking Versailles, seizing the Banque de France, or creating public property at the expense of the sacrosanct right of capitalist property, these same people start stammering. The Commune is not a simple repetition of 1789, it is the first workers' revolution in history."

Father was about to go one further when the bistro's cook rushed in to alert Lisa to the imminent arrival of a delegation from the Union des Femmes from Vaugirard.

"Karl, Jenny," she apologized, "I wish I could have spoken with you longer. I didn't even offer you a drink. What a shame! But the comrades will arrive any moment, and it would be wise …"

"Yes Lisa, of course," interrupted Moor. "We will leave right now. You can be proud of your actions. But please, take care. We will drink to your health after everything is finished. We promise!"

Father's faced betrayed his fears for her as he said these words of parting. The sight of the gun she slipped on her belt did not allay his fears. Nor did Lisa's reply to my questioning glance.

"Yes, as so many have done, I'm ready to die on a barricade in the days ahead!"

We thought about tiptoeing out of the place, but the boss decided otherwise and she sent us off with a ringing "Goodbye, Monsieur et Madame! Long live women and long live the Commune!"

5

A WALK THROUGH
INSURGENT PARIS

We left the Café des Nations around 8 a.m. Father was lost in his thoughts. I could tell that the interview with Lisa had made an impression on him; the Honorable Karl Marx was already impatient to put his ideas down on paper. For my part, my mood matched springtime in Paris, despite the tragic circumstances. Unbound by the tremendous stakes in this world, my heart had done just as it pleased and I had fallen in love all over again with Charles Longuet after our meeting. My soul was feverish, Moor's brain was on fire. We were standing there in front of the bistro, brooding over our thoughts. Our minds needed a break, to relax if only for a moment. I suggested that we wander through the streets with no particular destination in mind and breathe in the Parisian air that Victor Hugo claimed could restore one's soul.

"Moor, we've got plenty of time," I suggested. "Jean-François is picking us up in front of the Opera at noon. What if we took a walk?"

"Splendid idea, Jennychen!" Father replied cheerily. "I have been falling down in my fatherly duties. After all, you were born in Paris but you hardly know the city. Your mother and I were newlyweds when we moved to Rue Vanneau at the end of 1843. You were only a few months old when the French authorities expelled us in February 1845 under pressure from the Prussian ambassador. Our exile from Paris left a bitter taste, and it was all the more frustrating because we had come here precisely in order to express ourselves freely. In Cologne at the time, the atmosphere was unbreathable— the imperial authorities had just censored the *Rhineland Gazette*, of which I was the editor-in-chief because our liberal interpretation of Hegelian philosophy was considered subversive. My work on the newspaper, however, was only a rough draft of my ideas. It was here, on French soil, that my thoughts broke through their chrysalis and took flight. I had come to the capital hoping to perfect my ideas in the classrooms of the universal school of philosophy, I graduated from there with a diploma in revolutionary practice from the working-class neighborhoods of Paris. You might say, Jenny, that I too was born in Paris, at least in terms of politics. Let's walk to the docks. Let's not stick around here, the Place de la Corderie is close by and we risk coming across some familiar faces from the IWA who won't be fooled by my disguise for long!"

As we walked along Rue du Temple toward the Seine, I listened to Father recalling his years in Paris. Along the way, the shops opened up, displaying their wares along this old commercial street. It was the first time that Moor had confided in this way to me. I was absorbed by Father's melancholy, including his youthful infatuation with the Paris of the Enlightenment, whose intellectual bubbling had inspired his *Manuscripts*.[1] And he remembered working-class Paris too, that incarnation of communism, a thousand miles away from hair-brained philosophical incantations. He openly spoke of his personal disappointments as well, a rarity indeed, such as not being able to prolong his

---

1 Translator's note: *Marx's Economic and Philosophic Manuscripts of 1844.*

Parisian communist initiation. His story brought to light moments of doubt and exposed some deeply held regrets. Father was not inclined toward nostalgia; he forced himself to maintain a certain distance from the past, sharing only what his modesty permitted. The sound of his voice soothed me and helped explain the images of Paris slowly passing before my eyes. I opened and closed my eyelids, hoping to imprint every detail. The worn-down cobblestones, eroded by time, seemed to be begging the gas lamps, themselves in bad shape, to cast a bit more light their way. Here and there, brand-new sewer covers reminded us that the city had tamed the wastewaters that had dominated it for so long. In the distance a stone staircase, narrow and snaking along with a wrought iron railing, held back precarious walls on either side so as not to disappear into a dark passage. Less preoccupied with the future, a newly inaugurated square stood ready to welcome all the kids who would soon come frolicking from all directions, playing among the swings, the bandstand, and the merry-go-round.

Father continued his story as I savored the moment. Paris was rising, standing tall on firm footing. A line of women in aprons were waiting to be hired on the steps of a textile workshop. A washhouse stood across the street sheltered beneath a stocky frame; a din emanated from within, stifled by mounds of linen under vigorous attack by figures covered in shawls and scarves. Further down, the street was crowded with people. National Guard battalions blocked the street while wheelbarrows, overflowing with coal, crowded the sidewalks. Hearty men in blue jackets dutifully shoveled the precious cargo into an oven through the cellar duct of a building. A swarm of street urchins, *les Gavroches*, came out of nowhere, surrounding us, determined to extract a few pennies. Next came the newspaper boys, whose cheeky banter left us no other choice but to buy their editions: "News of the day! Who wants *Le Père Duchesne, Le Vengeur, Le Cri du Peuple*?[2] Versailles held at bay, the Commune conquers!" Frontpage satirical carica-tures rivaled each other to sketch Adolphe Thiers in ever more compromising poses. Father bought a copy of each paper without once interrupting his monologue. At the corner of Rue de Rivoli, we were almost run over by two Red Cross ambulances racing at full speed. The war reasserted itself.

"Jenny, you know," murmured Moor, "all these injuries, all these deaths…"

On the Place de l'Hôtel de Ville, Father and I were killing time in front of the Commune's headquarters as we hoped to be able to meet Varlin there very soon. The building shook at its habitual boiling point. The sun showed down on the stone quays along Grève, enthroned in the middle of the Île de la Cité,[3] which was almost deserted. The Arcole Bridge glowed in all its brilliance, enveloped in a sparkling halo that evoked the singular clarity captured by Camille Pissarro in his paintings. But Father saw the scene from a different perspective.

"They destroyed everything. This district used to be full of in-habitants, at least twenty thousand people. A labyrinth of narrow streets and blocks of houses, from the courthouse to the cathe-dral. What happened to all these people? There's just this mili-tary barracks. Even the Hôtel-Dieu has been rebuilt."

"Yes, the work of Baron Haussmann."[4]

---

2   Translator's note: Three radical newspapers.

3   Translator's note: An island in the river Seine in the middle of Paris.

4   Translator's note: Emperor Napoleon III ordered Georges-Eugène Haussmann, the prefect of Paris, to renovate Paris after the revo-lution of 1848 by tearing down working-class neighborhoods and replacing crooked streets with wide boulevards.

I leaned on the parapet to rest my feet while Moor inspected the damage up close. The Seine, too, was congested: boats, canoes and a number of shaky crafts were sailing up and down, obviously without the benefit of a compass. This squalid flotilla was trying to load a few reckless passengers, some abandoned animals, and containers loaded with wheat, all the while struggling to stay afloat. It must be said that supplies in the capital were lacking. The noose had loosened somewhat since the January armistice with the Germans, but the relief had been short-lived. Famine stalked the streets once more, although the danger was less acute than during the Prussian siege. The Communards remained rather silent on this subject. However, we knew that the end of the year had been particularly tragic. The instinct for survival had overridden any concerns about the contents of their meals, and hunger had forced more than one to swallow—eyes closed and hearts heavy—horse, dog, and cat meat. Field mice and rats were all that was left for the poorest of the poor. Not even the catastrophe of hunger escaped the sacred laws of the class struggle. The bourgeoisie, for its part, had feasted during Christmas in the capital's upscale restaurants, paying top price, of course, to dine on "consommé d'éléphant" as Castor and Pollux, the Jardin des Plantes zoo's prize pachyderms, were served up on the menu. Four months had passed since the German blockade had ended, but Thiers had picked up where Bismarck left off. Once again, Paris subsisted on black bread.

Father wanted to stay on the right bank. We therefore resumed our journey across the quays to Place du Châtelet. Father couldn't believe it.

"They moved the Column! How did these two theaters spring from the ground in such a short time? Jenny, this is absolutely amazing! The avenue goes on as far as the eye can see."

"Yes, Father, it's the Boulevard Sébastopol, Baron Haussmann is at it again."

The Empire had reconfigured Paris from top to bottom in record time and demolished many popular districts. Haussmann's boulevards now pierced the capital from north to south and east to west, connecting the city gates to the center. Louis Bonaparte had taken particular care of the Parisian bourgeoisie by building them tailor-made homes, tall stone buildings, recognizable among all. Only the top floor and the attic were reserved for small staffs. Obviously, the aristocrats had saved their private mansions in the Faubourg Saint-Germain. But Paris had been emptied of its tumultuous people and its revolts. The workers and the poor were driven out of the center to live mainly in the new arrondissements annexed to Paris by Thiers in 1860: Les Batignolles, Montmartre, and Belleville.

"Yes, Jennychen," intoned Moor, "A real counter-revolution. And Haussmann planted a time bomb in the public budget before resigning, last year, under duress. The famous 'fantastic accounts' of Baron Haussmann, as Jules Ferry likes to joke. The indebtedness created by the cost of these pharaonic works will explode sooner or later. Just as it has done elsewhere, real estate speculation made capitalists believe that they could create money out of money. Their delusions will be shattered, crashing headlong into reality. The infinite accumulation of this fictitious capital is only one of the symptoms of economic crisis, the mechanism of which I tried to dismantle in my book *Capital*. But you knew this before anyone else. It was all in my 'endless' book, as you liked to say, which you complained took up all my time."

"Fortunately, you couldn't bring all of your notes with you, otherwise we would never have been able to enjoy our walk!"

"You are not wrong, Jennychen. And that would have been very regrettable. Paris is unrecognizable. It makes me dizzy. The productive capacities poured into this urban reorganization say a lot about the potentials that accompany the rise of the bourgeoisie. At the same time, these long boulevards may pose a problem for the Commune as they may be more advantageous for Versailles' cannons than the insurgents' barricades."

As he walked, Father took in this new Paris with an air of fascination and disdain.

The Louvre Palace proudly displayed the colors of the Commune. A banner, hung from a pontoon, announcing an assembly of the Federation of Artists of Paris, which was to vote that same day on establishing an executive committee. Several hundred people were gathered on the museum platform.

"Father, that man over there, is that Gustave Courbet?"

"Yes, it's probably him. Eugène Pottier must also be there."

A young man who looked like a revolutionary artist came over to offer us a fine brochure. Elegantly dressed, he cultivated false bohemian airs in his immaculate peasant shirt and brown velvet jacket.

"Good evening, citizens. Would you like a copy of our manifesto?"

"With pleasure. Is this the Commune's cultural program?"

"In a way," replied the artist. "But our federation is careful not to insist on any one 'truth' with respect to the matter. We do not seek to proclaim an official art. On the contrary, we demand 'the free expression of art, free from any government tutelage and all privileges.' Culture should never become an instrument of domination, or a commodity. As you know, when the winds of emancipation come up, they blow in all directions. I am an actor, I work with a lyric troupe and our company has never flourished as we are now. We pool our creations in spontaneous exhibitions, or what we call spectacles, which can be held in public squares or in the former Empire's buildings, or sometimes even inside churches. Many private theaters have been transformed into cooperatives. The Commune gives young designers the opportunity to expand their talent. Paintings, sculptures, engravings, literature, poetry, and songs, whatever it may be, our revolution is brimming with talent."

"What relations do you maintain with the Commune?" I asked.

"Our destinies are intertwined. Our federation, when it was formed not long ago, made a point of reminding us that we belong to the Commune, even while preserving our autonomy. Our goal remains 'artists should govern the world of art,' but there is a perfect harmony between us. Projects are flourishing in every arrondissement. We aim to put our motto, 'communal luxury,' within everyone's reach. Education is also necessary in order to incorporate creation as part of shared and taught knowledge. We have proposed providing art education in preschools. The Commune's great innovation, which differentiates it from bourgeois art, is to bring the creativity of craftsmen, stonemasons, leather cutters, carvers, jewelers, and even upholsterers, into the ranks of artistic creation. But I see that our meeting is about to begin; I must go. It was a pleasure talking to you!"

We thanked him warmly for his explanations and then exchanged a knowing and amused glance when we discovered that he had slipped one of his poems between the pages of the artist union's pamphlet as a bookmark.

At that moment, a young man with a lively gaze and a beautiful teenage face approached us.

"I see you are interested in poetry," he commented, with a slightly ironic smile.

"What can poetry do for a revolution like this one?" Moor asked innocently.

The young stranger replied without hesitation, "A pen in hand is worth a hand at the plow."

Father was amazed by the answer but found it suggestive. Attracted by the intense and wistful gaze of the young poet, I also wanted to ask him a question.

"What is, in your opinion, the purpose of the Commune?"

"To change life!" he shot back, as if he were throwing a stick of dynamite.

Father thought for a moment, then replied, "Wouldn't it be better to say to transform the world?"

"Couldn't we combine both ideas?" I said when it was my turn to speak.

Our young friend seemed satisfied with this conclusion, but he was in a hurry to leave for the artists' assembly. Curious, I asked him his name.

"Arthur," he responded laconically.

"Arthur who?" I insisted.

"Rimbaud," he said, before disappearing into the crowd.

After walking along the building, we turned up the Rue Saint-Honoré before reaching the crossroads of the Rue des Bons-Enfants where Father stopped dead.

"Jenny," he said with a start, "let's take a detour. I would like to check something."

We walked to number 20.

"No," he said excitedly. "They didn't demolish everything. Jenny, this is where we had our meetings with the League of the Just, right here at the Café Scherger. Believe me, the debates could go on until the morning. This circle of German socialist workers, most of whom were in exile as we were, immediately adopted me. A few had participated in the failed insurrection of 1839 alongside Blanqui, to whom they were close at the time. This grouping was the basis upon which we founded the Communist League years later in 1847."

Once we passed through the Palais-Royal garden, we came to Rue des Petits-champs and then on to the corner of Rue des Moulins.

"These are the premises of *Vorwärts*, the newspaper in which I participated after working on the *Annales franco-allemandes*. Right there on the first floor, every day, we had editorial board meetings that were more like political assemblies. That's where my political friendship with Engels was sealed. The revolution, the proletariat, relations of property, Babeuf, so many words and names must have echoed off those walls a thousand times."

At this stage of our walk, I must admit, we almost got lost in a huge construction site, before finally finding Jean-François in front of the Opera House. Or more precisely, in front of the new Opera House, whose construction had begun fifteen years earlier under the leadership of a fashionable architect named Garnier, but which had been suspended due to the war. Hidden behind a rickety scaffolding, the main facade displayed nothing more than the building's steps and an imposing pediment decorated with friezes. Swirls of dust whipped around us. While Father brushed off his jacket, I gazed at the luxurious bistro in front of us, the café at the Grand Hôtel de la Paix. Even in the midst of a civil war, the Grands Boulevards were still the Grands Boulevards. Bistros, restaurants, and theaters competed with one another for preeminence. Until March, anyone who was anybody preened and paraded in this posh part of town, but now they had packed their

bags and left. All the furs, fine suits, and silk dresses had disappeared, probably decamped to Versailles. However, the proletarians who had since taken possession of the premises appeared to
be honoring the district's traditions by taking care to dress up
before coming to tread down these lofty boulevards.

Bewitched by the sights, neither Father nor I had noticed that
a rough carriage, drawn by two valiant horses, had parked next to
us. Its driver, seated on a large bench, was watching us mockingly.
It was Jean-François.

"So, you have fallen under Paris's spell?" he chuckled. "Hop
on, my friends, I am making a delivery for work. Before I take
you back to Léo's, I have to detour to a depot not far from here to
pick up a few crates that I absolutely need for tomorrow morning."

We did not ask any questions, only too happy to continue
our excursion. Thus, our unlikely team set off up the Boulevard
des Capucines. After the Madeleine church, we turned onto Rue
Boissy-d'Anglas and then came to a porte-cochère, a covered en-
tryway as dilapidated as it was narrow. Jean-François maneuvered
his trailer to the back of the courtyard in order to park it as close
as possible to the workshop. A sturdy man with broad shoulders
and a weathered face approached us. The sleeves of his gray blouse
were rolled up to the elbows, and he had a pencil stuck to his ear.

"Hi, Jean-François," said the man.

"Joseph, how are you? I have come to pick up my shipment, if
it's ready. Let me introduce you to my friends who are passing
through Paris."

"Delighted to meet you, citizens, welcome to our cabinetmak-
ing and carpentry cooperative."

I was immediately seized by the uproar inside the factory. A
mechanical sawblade shrieked incessantly, but it didn't prevent

the dozen or so workers present from noticing our arrival; they all waved a friendly hello to us. A suffocating heat permeated the modest factory and its glass roof concentrated the smell of wood glue, saturating the air. Planks, saws, nails, hammers, metal bars, and several leather saddlebags filled with all kinds of tools lay on the cement floor lined with shavings.

"Here they are, my friend, your boxes are stored at the back on the branch," said the woodworker.

"Thanks, Joseph. Is the work going alright?" asked Jean-François.

"We're holding on, we've been able to pay the bills for two weeks."

Father, intrigued by this information, joined the conversation.

"Do you really work as a cooperative?" he asked.

"Absolutely. We didn't have much choice, the owner scampered off like a rabbit as soon as the plebs took charge. But we weren't born yesterday and we prevented him from taking the stockpile of lumber he had bought with business' funds. Since then, we are paid at the end of each week, making wooden crates for Léo's establishment, boxes for transporting National Guard weapons, and wine barrels, too. Those are tricky enough! But we have good lads here and we have had to innovate. We used to specialize in wooden trunks, especially fancy ones used by those who travel by coach. With all the bigwigs that came to stay at the Hôtel Crillon just next door, we had plenty of customers, let me tell you! But they're gone now, so we're using the wood for different jobs."

"How do you distribute the earnings from your work?" asked Moor.

"Equally, of course! Right since we started. We take stock all together every weekend and every day a commission, composed of three elected members, manages the workshop's affairs. We have also set up a common fund for transportation. Some of us live nearby, but others, like me, come from further afield. I live in Levallois with my wife Berthe and my brother, who is a textile worker. Finding one of the horse-drawn omnibuses and getting past the fortifications is no picnic. Especially since the Versaillese bomb us until we're deaf!"

"Do you manage everything yourselves?" continued Father.

"Yes. Orders, manufacturing projects, sales, cash flow. Everything," Joseph replied proudly. "We don't miss a thing. We even brought the Commune a few valuables that we've patched up, some precious ceramic vases or expensive crockery that certain families from the luxury Crillon apartments left us because they were chipped or broken. We had some pieces appraised, and even though we fixed them up, they were still worth their weight in gold. The hardest thing is knowing how to anticipate and calculate expenses. Fortunately, we work with comrades from the other unions; we help each other and share our skills. And it's a good thing too. You see, we mostly learned to speak and sometimes to write in the revolutionary clubs, but not really to count! Alright, I'll have to go back, take care of yourself. And Jean-François, say hello to Léo. See you soon and long live the Commune!"

After loading the order and securing it, we set off again. Moor apparently had a final request which he whispered mysteriously into Jean-François's ear while I concentrated on the capital's landscape: the Place de la Concorde, with its statue of Strasbourg, now covered with a large black cloth since the annexation of Alsace and Lorraine by the Prussians; the bridge; the Orsay quay; then the Esplanade des Invalides. A few minutes later, our makeshift vehicle slowed down on Rue Vanneau, before stopping in front of number 38.

"This, Jennychen," winked Father, "is where we lived, this is where you were born."

That night, Father was particularly tired, but he seemed pleased and cheerful. During supper, he gave Léo a detailed assessment of our day, without forgetting to inquire about the possible availability of Eugène Varlin and Louise Michel over the coming days. Then he went to bed and fell fast asleep, a well-deserved night's rest.

6

EUGÈNE VARLIN

ANTI-AUTHORITARIAN COMMUNIST

Léo informed Eugène Varlin, his collaborator at the Finance Commission, of Moor's visit. The next day, we were invited to meet him at his office at the Hôtel de Ville. We had met Varlin at the London Congress of the International in 1865. He was a young workman, a bookbinder by trade, tall, with thick black hair pushed back and a plentiful beard. His bright black eyes expressed kindness and energy. At the party organized to celebrate the IWA's first anniversary, he made me and my sisters, Laura and Tussy, dance! He spoke only French but, unlike some of his compatriots, was not effusive, speaking soberly and precisely.

Father had the greatest respect for him. "Varlin is not a Proudhonist like the others. A brilliant organizer, he has succeeded in uniting the workers' associations of Paris in a federation and bringing them into the International. During the government's prosecutions against the Internationalists, he made a magnificent speech, denouncing capitalism and the 'financial pashas who create abundance or scarcity at will, sowing lies, ruin, and bankruptcy all the while with the millions they accumulate.' I can quote it from memory. We succeeded, thanks to him, in neutralizing the 'individualist' Proudhonists at the Basel Congress in 1869 and approved a collectivist resolution for the socialization of land ownership. Our main opponent in this controversy, Monsieur Tolain, has lately shown his true colors by choosing the Versaillese over the Commune."

I hastened to add my two cents to Father's homage, recalling that he had the courage to defend women's right to work against his Proudhonist friends and to advocate for the principle of "equal pay for equal work."

Next Léo, who did not try to hide the esteem in which he held his internationalist friend, quoted a passage from Varlin's defense on May 22, 1868, before the Empire's judges. "Only a wind of absolute freedom can purify this atmosphere so rife with iniquities and heavy with future storms."

According to Léo, Varlin had foreseen, like a prophet of new times, the tempest that would break out in Paris three years later. And were that not enough, he had taken part in the uprising of March 18 at the head of the Batignolles National Guard that launched the Commune. He always stood out for his decisive spirit, his boldness, his courage, and his humanity. As a result, he quickly became very popular; during the elections for the Commune, he was the only candidate to have been elected by three different arrondissements: the 6th, 12th, and 17th.

The following day we went to meet him at the Hôtel de Ville. An enormous red flag was draped across the magnificent Renaissance facade of this historic building, the political heart of the Commune. Detachments of the National Guard and a few of their cannons were stationed all around, standing guard over this strategic site. Guards, rifles on the shoulder, controlled the entrances and it was necessary to have a pass drawn up by the district councils, by the battalions of the Guard, or by the Commune's elected officials, to be admitted. Ours, written out in the names of "Mr. and Miss Richardson, English merchants," was countersigned by Léo Frankel. Just in front of us, a dubious-looking character, without any clear rationale for doing so, was trying hard to make his way through, but the resolute guards stopped him in his tracks. An altercation ensued, but the individual eventually gave up and left, grumbling. Thanks to Léo's pass, we were admitted without a hitch, and the guards even gave us a smile.

Intense agitation enveloped the building: armed guards, workers, and messengers were running in all directions; discussions filled the corridors with small groups forming to exchange information. We noticed a few women as well, most likely activists from the Union des Femmes pour la défense de Paris. The Hôtel de Ville was a beehive, buzzing constantly. Was this joyous disorder merely an outer appearance, or was it an essential characteristic of this popular insurrection?

Varlin was waiting for us on the first floor in his office at the Finance Commission. It was one of those rooms in the Hôtel de Ville decorated in spectacular Third Empire style, an artificial luxury contrasted notably with the simple table and chairs, which might have come from the humble cabinetmakers we met from Faubourg Saint-Honoré.

Varlin was delighted, but very surprised, when he saw us arrive.

"Citizen Marx," he exclaimed. "You are unrecognizable! Your disguise is perfect!"

"Congratulations are owed to my daughter, Jenny, Citizen Varlin," Moor replied, grinning. "She was the one who invented this subterfuge."

"Well done, citizen, you have shown commendable prudence."

Now, it was my turn to greet him.

"Dear Eugene, it is a great pleasure to see you again. I have never forgotten our waltz at the International party in London."

After this opening, Father got right to the heart of the matter.

"Citizen Varlin, I must admit that I am deeply impressed by what is happening here in Paris. Though hungry, and disrupted more by inner betrayal than by the outer enemy, Paris has courageously risen up. What resilience, what historic initiative, what capacity for sacrifice! History knows no other example of such greatness! The Commune is the most glorious achievement of our party since the Parisian June insurrection."

"Hopefully it will not end like in 1848!" replied Varlin, smiling wryly.

At this point, Moor's attention was drawn to a colorful poster from the Commune, which had replaced the portrait of the Emperor above the fireplace, probably sent to the dump. He approached the wall to study it. The poster depicted a Fédéré—as the volunteers to the National Guard in 1792 were known—behind a cannon, waving a red flag with the motto "La Commune ou la Mort" with a woman at his side wearing a Phrygian cap. She was pointing her arm toward a town that could be seen in the distance. The title of the poster left no doubt as to its meaning, "On to Versailles!"

Father looked at Varlin once again with a big smile.

"This poster is right! You were too kind, you should have marched on Versailles straight away. You did not want to start the civil war, but hasn't this runt Thiers already started it by trying to disarm Paris?"

Varlin shared his opinion. He told Moor that during the first few days he had advocated the Commune going on the offensive. The problem was that, if the National Guard (made up of good, dignified, and courageous people) represented the people in arms, it was not a professional army. The Guard lacked discipline and, despite the efforts of the Commissioner of War Gustave Cluseret, was not used to conducting operations on a battlefield.

A little uneasy with this response, Father approached the question from another angle. In his opinion, the Commune needed someone like Blanqui, capable of correcting the situation and of disciplining the combatants, and he wondered if there was some way to win his release.

Varlin explained to him that, following the assassination of Duval and Flourens by the Versaillese, the Commune had taken a few dozen hostages, including the Archbishop of Paris, Monseigneur Darboy, and had offered to exchange this illustrious cleric for Blanqui. But Thiers had categorically refused, and the Commune was now going to offer to exchange all its hostages for Auguste Blanqui alone.

More than a little skeptical of this working, Moor asked, "And what if he refuses? Are you going to execute the hostages?"

Varlin gasped, "Never! I would oppose it with all my might. That would violate our socialist principles.[1] By doing so, we would give our enemies an excuse to accuse us of wanting to revive the Terror of 1793. Blanqui's release would be magnificent, but I do not believe that a single individual can change our precarious military situation."

Moor pressed his point, again pointing to the poster above the fireplace; wasn't the National Guard capable of leading an offensive?

---

1   Editors' Note: During the Bloody Week of May 25, Varlin unsuccessfully opposed the execution of hostages on Rue Haxo. The Versaillese did not display the same generosity of spirit; three days later, he was captured and shot by order of the generals.

Varlin doubted such a possibility, reminding Father that the Guard had attempted an attack against the Versaillese in Châtillon on April 3, but the Communards had been defeated. The Versaillese took one thousand National Guards prisoner along with two of the Commune's best commanders, Duval and Flourens, who were both executed.

Growing increasingly concerned, Moor then asked Varlin how the Commune was planning to confront Thiers's troops. Varlin hesitated for a few moments. It wasn't an easy question to answer. Finally, he offered us a realistic hypothesis.

"Our battalions are rooted in the popular neighborhoods. Their method of spontaneous struggle is that of all the popular insurgencies in our history: the barricade. If the Versaillese attack us, Paris will bristle with barricades, each with its cannon. The National Guard will fight courageously. Versailles will meet fierce resistance."

Father was only half convinced. How could barricades resist an attack from the regular army?

"Our hope is that the scenes from March 18 will be repeated when the frontline soldiers refused to shoot the people, they hoisted their rifle butts in the air and fired at their own Generals," offered Varlin.

"What if that doesn't happen, Citizen Varlin?" countered Father.

"Then it will be a bloodbath, much worse than June 1848, Citizen Marx."

A silence fell as each of us reflected on this sincere but disturbing exchange. Moor then raised another concern. In his opinion, the National Guard's Central Committee had wasted too much time by relinquishing its power and organizing elections to the Commune. Revolutionaries had an excessive concern for "honesty!"

Varlin did not agree. His answer was clear and precise.

"Dear Marx," he retorted. "Revolutionaries are never too honest! Elections were essential to ensure the legitimacy of the insurgency. They guarantee that the Commune effectively represents the people of Paris. On this point, we all agreed in the Central Committee of the Guard: the Proudhonists, the Blanquists, the Jacobins, and the social republicans."

I didn't say anything, but I think Varlin was right. Father didn't look convinced, but he didn't insist, preferring to change the subject. Why had the Commune's Finance Committee not taken over the Banque de France?

Our interlocutor searched briefly for some documents in his drawer, which he consulted before answering us.

"Here, you are right," Varlin replied. "I agree with you. I proposed it to the Central Committee of the National Guard, but my advice was not followed. We therefore sent an ultimatum to the governor of the Banque de France, demanding the immediate payment of one million francs for our National Guards' salaries. I went with Jourde, the financial specialist from the Guard, to the bank's headquarters and we got what we demanded. And we will go return whenever our needs require …"

"Yes, but at the same time, the Bank is paying tens, if not hundreds of millions to Versailles," interrupted Father.

"It's true, but I cannot override my mandate from the Commune."

Just then came a knock on the door and a National Guard entered. He explained to Varlin that two Communards, Citizens Grelier and Viard, had gathered a considerable quantity of silverware in the 11th arrondissement's town hall—confiscated by the people in the palaces and churches—and they were asking what to do with the treasure.

Thanking the guard for this information, Varlin hastily wrote out a message that he asked him to take to these two intrepid comrades. This precious booty would be transferred as quickly as possible to the mint, where Citizen Camélinat would melt it down into silver coins without delay. The Commune really needed it!

Once the messenger left with the instructions, our friend turned to us, his face beaming. "You see, this is the people of Paris! No theft, no looting, no individuals 'recovering' property for themselves. The silverware of the rich fugitives and the parasitic clergy has been brought to the officials of the National Guard or to the district councils and is under guard in the 11th arrondissement. Soon we will have some shiny silver coins in circulation."

Father replied admiringly, but also with a touch of irony, "It seems that all the citizens of this insurgent city know the International Workingmens' Association's collectivist resolutions by heart!"

"Quite the contrary," responded Varlin. "But the people are spontaneously collectivist."

Father wanted to know what influence the International held over the Commune. Varlin explained to him that the socialists and internationalists were only a minority, but they were listened to. Most of the members of the Commune Assembly were Jacobins or social republicans.

At this point, Moor could not resist, he had wanted to question his interlocutor right from the start about his political views.

"Allow me to ask a personal question, Citizen Varlin," began Father. "What is your orientation with regard to socialist doctrine? Are you still a Proudhonist? Do you have any affinities with Bakunin? You voted for his proposal to abolish the right of inheritance at the Basel IWA conference, after all."

A little taken aback by Moor's somewhat indiscreet request, Varlin pretended to rummage through the papers on his table to buy a little time. Finally, he replied with a slightly ironic smile.

"My dear friend, I am not a man taken by doctrines. I am just a humble worker bee, who makes my honey from many flowers. I greatly admire your writings and those of your friend Friedrich Engels. You have exposed the hypocrisy of bourgeois economists who reduced social science to market considerations alone, all in the name of so-called economic freedom. You have demonstrated, irrefutably, the inequity of our economic system based on the immense accumulation of capital on one side, and the misery of the workers on the other. However, I also find interesting ideas in Fourier, Proudhon, and Bakunin's work. You know I founded a popular canteen, the Marmite, and ran it for many years. I use our doctrines just like I cook in my kitchen; I try to integrate and combine all the socialist ingredients, adding them in my own special sauce. I consider myself to be a collectivist socialist or a nonauthoritarian communist."

This answer was good enough for Moor.

"I am happy to drum up business, dear Varlin, for your Communist Marmite! May the people nourish themselves on your tasty cuisine! But tell me, dear friend, what might we do, once back in London, to help the Commune?"

Varlin paused to consider this offer. The proposal was interesting but required some caution. After a few moments, he turned to Father and made two requests. First, the Commune had confiscated bonds worth a few million francs in the National Bank. Could Moor try to trade them on the London Stock Exchange?[2] Second, Varlin asked his friend to write, based on his impressions during this visit, a new address on behalf of the IWA in solidarity with the Commune. Father assured him that he would do his best to fulfill these requests. In his eyes, it was the least he could do for the Commune, the cause of the international proletariat.

I then spoke up to address a subject that was close to my heart.

"Dear Eugene, you who were one of the first French trade unionists to demand equal pay for women and men, according to the principle of 'equal pay for equal work.' What can you do to ensure the Commune takes up this basic demand for social justice?"

It was an issue with which Varlin felt quite at ease and he answered me with great sincerity. He had met a lot of resistance from his comrades on this question, and not only from "narrow" Proudhonists. However, he had convinced them to take a first step, that is, equal pay for teachers. He hoped to be able to make further progress on this delicate ground, but that would depend to a large extent on the ability of women themselves to organize and fight for their rights. He reported that Nathalie Le Mel had told him that the issue was already being discussed in the Union des Femmes.

Moor spoke up again. This time his tone was serious and a little solemn. He admitted that Varlin's assessment of the military situation greatly troubled him and that he feared for the

---

2   Editors' Note: Marx's attempt to interest the British Stock Exchange in these bonds was unsuccessful.

future of this wonderful experience. He was convinced that any negotiations were impossible; the bourgeois scoundrels in power at Versailles would leave the Commune only one choice: to resist or to capitulate without a fight.

This time Varlin didn't hesitate. His response was immediate and categorical.

"Dear Marx, whatever happens, I can assure you that the Commune will not capitulate without resistance. The people of Paris will fight relentlessly, barricade by barricade, arrondissement by arrondissement, until the last cartridge. Our sacred slogan is, and will remain, 'La Commune ou la Mort!'"

"I believe you," replied Father. "Thanks to the Commune, the struggle of the working class against the capitalist class and its state has entered a new phase. Whatever the outcome of your struggle, we have obtained a new starting point of universal historic significance."

"You have summed up the meaning of our struggle perfectly…"

A new silence hung in the air before Varlin spoke again.

"Who have you already met in Paris, besides our friend Frankel?"

Father mentioned Elisabeth Dmitrieff, whose name immediately sparked Varlin's enthusiasm.

"What an admirable woman! What courage, what energy, what intelligence! Léo and I both fell in love with her! Who are you meeting with next?"

Moor explained we were going to see Louise Michel presently and he took the opportunity to ask Varlin for a pass for her Club. Taking out his best pen, our friend promptly provided us with the requested document. We took our leave, embracing one another, overcome by emotion. I couldn't contain my tears.

I took detailed notes of this deeply sincere, humane, and warm exchange between Moor and Eugène Varlin. But we left the Hôtel de Ville with a heavy heart, worried about the Commune's fate.

7

MEETING WITH LOUISE MICHEL

We stayed around Léo's house the next morning and Father made some notes. As for me, I was particularly excited to meet Louise Michel in the 18th arrondissement in the late afternoon. Eugène Varlin, whom we had just met, had served as an intermediary. At the stroke of 1 p.m., Jean-François arrived and was once again ready to help. Always so attentive, he kindly offered to take us.

"Karl, Jenny, if you feel like it, we can leave now and we can wander around a bit. Your 'coach' is ready. But be warned, you must go along with the route I chose. It's non-negotiable!"

He had burst out laughing. The idea of making these demands on Marx seemed to amuse him. I glanced at Father, who seemed delighted with Jean-François's stipulations. Our guide, always lively, bowed theatrically on the front steps of the house to let us know that he intended to play his role until the end.

"Get a move on, M'ssieu, Dame. Let's go!" he joked. "If we had had all day, I would have started with Denfert square in the 14th arrondissement to show you the Catacombes, but you'd probably prefer to stay above ground, wouldn't you?"

He laughed again. To the right on Place d'Italie, we took Boulevard de l'Hôpital de la Salpêtrière past the quays at the Jardin des Plantes. A gigantic covered market considerably enlarged the Austerlitz station. We crossed the Seine and went up through the Canal Saint-Martin basin to the Bastille. Father rubbed his knee mechanically with the palm of his hand, drinking from a small bottle of whey. The square was crowded with people. Street vendors shouted above the din, selling their trinkets. They yelled over one another in hopes of outdoing the competition and being heard over heated discussions about the price of bread. Some argued bitterly and I wondered if a fight would break out, yet Father appeared relaxed and seemed acclimated to the Parisian proletarians' customs.

"The working-class culture here is hot-headed. Workers here know how to carve stone, produce articles for union newspapers, and some even write poems. But they also like to speak loudly and use the most expressive gestures," he explained.

The human tide engulfed us as we approached Boulevard Saint-Antoine. Bumbling along, we made our way between the delivery men who stocked up the shops with tapestries, wallpaper, or stones. The workshops went on endlessly. Father was gathering his thoughts. This boulevard had been his favorite place in 1844 because it had a number of exiled German workers who had, moreover, earned solid reputations for not allowing themselves to be pushed around. They took part in all the strikes and all the Parisian insurgencies—the "bears" of the Faubourg Saint-Antoine, as Engels nicknamed them.

Jean-François avoided the Place du Trône, which was under the National Guard, and continued our journey in the direction of Père-Lachaise. A compact funeral procession blocked our progress for several minutes as it made its way up the Rue de la Roquette before turning into the cemetery. The crowd, dressed entirely in black, had come to bury their dead. The silent parade stretched as far as the eye could see, lined up behind dozens of coffins covered with red flags. The people of Paris followed the victims' families to the edge of the common grave. A marching band brought up the rear of the march, playing a melodious hymn. The whole scene filled me with emotion.

"You know, with each passing day, we mourn our own and do our best to pay them homage with dignity," explained one of the mourners. "Two weeks ago, hundreds of thousands of us marched here from the Hôpital Beaujon. Versailles will pay for this infamy one way or another."

As we watched, a deep sorrow fell over us. Eventually, we got on our way, leaving the funeral procession behind. None of us said a word until we reached Ménilmontant. When we got to the Belleville neighborhood, I could barely make out Father muttering under his breath, "Belleville and Cabet's first communist banquets were held here."

To lighten the mood, our faithful guide took it upon himself to introduce us to the capital's new curiosity, namely, the Buttes-Chaumont park. This green space had been entirely constructed over abandoned gypsum mineral quarries. I found the juxtaposition of the countryside to the city only some meters away somewhat uncanny.

As our horse trotted on, our improvised stagecoach finally reached the Butte-Montmartre, where it had all started on March 18. Then, after having crisscrossed many alleys, some of them covered in vines, we turned back down to the Goutte d'Or district.

It was not quite 5 p.m. when Jean-François parked his carriage halfway up the Rue de la Chapelle in front of the "Justice" Committee. He then took his leave of us, but not before discreetly suggesting that he could wait at a nearby café for our meeting with

Louise Michel to end as he thought Moor seemed a bit worn out. I declined his kind offer because I didn't want to abuse his generosity any longer. Father and I managed to elbow our way through the fifty or so people gathered at the front door. A red fabric banner covered with black letters reading "Club de la Révolution" hung from the building. When it was our turn, I went up to the four women guarding the entrance, weapons hanging from their belts. After greeting them, I handed over the letter from Eugène Varlin recommending us to Citizen Michel. The bravest of the group immediately snatched up the letter without taking her eyes off Moor, staring at him disapprovingly; obviously she thought something was not quite right.

We were at a women's club, and not just any women's club, but that of the 18th arrondissement, whose reputation so worried Versailles. But just at that precise moment, a terrible doubt seized me as to the relevance of our meeting place. Why choose this committee rather than the one led by Théophile Ferré at 41 Chaussée de Clignancourt, which was mainly reserved for men? Louise Michel participated in two assemblies every day, at least until the fighting called her to the barricades. There was therefore no obstacle to meeting with her on Ferré's terrain. But Varlin had been categorical: Father's presence would arouse less suspicion in the women's club than mine would in the one dominated by men. So I accepted his decision and cast our lot in with his intuition, crossing my fingers that his "open sesame" would get us through the door.

After endless back and forth between the sentry box and an office which apparently made all the decisions, the female guard finally let us pass. The better part of the resistance to Moor being allowed to pass was now appeased, and the guard even apologized for the zeal with which she carried out her duties. We had no complaints, however, about her wholly legitimate vigilance. A young girl with a jovial face and flushed cheeks then invited us to sit in a small room which overlooked the street. A few minutes later, she came back to offer us something to quench our thirst while awaiting Citizen Louise Michel's arrival, who, it turned out, might be a little late. The point was clear, we were going to have to grin and bear it. As the clock ticked, we became resigned in silence to the fact that the meeting might not take place. I supposed that Father, like me, was questioning the merits of our incessant requests for discussions with all these Communards who had more urgent matters to attend to than to answer our questions and entertain our hypotheses. Such were the limitations of our secret visit to Paris. Political precautions prevented us from getting involved in Parisian life because Versailles might use our supposed "interference" to discredit the Commune, a consideration that had almost prevented us from crossing the Channel in the first place. This status of perpetual witness frustrated my desire to join in Parisian life and especially to fight. But above all else, neither Father nor I wanted to rob the revolutionaries of the precious time of the alliance.

Moor was about to give up when we heard the squealing brakes of a horse-drawn carriage which rekindled our hope. It was Louise Michel! Her rapid descent from the coachman's seat indicated that she was a woman in a hurry. However, her gestures did not betray any haste. She aimed to master the rhythm of time even when it tried to escape her. Every moment counted, which is why, before she did anything else, she passed several unhurried seconds showing her gratitude for the horses, gently stroking their manes. Then, closely followed by an armed woman, she strode toward the guards. Everyone then embraced, as if it was a long-awaited reunion.

Notwithstanding her frail physique, Louise Michel's figure exuded an imposing presence. It was hard to describe—a kind of benevolent power and natural aura emanated from her spontaneously. Many things have been said about her, but I have to say that the typical description of her as an austere school teacher, customarily sporting a black blouse, absolutely failed to capture the woman we had the pleasure of meeting that day. Nor did the commonplace portrayals of her as "the Red Virgin" or of the "Joan of Arc of the Revolution" that narrow minds peddled about her; instead, a genuine National Guard was about to join us. Her kepi military cap was screwed down tight on her head, her uniform had obviously seen its share of combat, and she sported a Remington rifle slung over her shoulder. Once the hugs ended, one of her acolytes leaned over to whisper a few words in her ear. She immediately turned and marched in our direction, limping distinctly.

"Good day to you," she said, greeting us warmly. "Forgive me for this inconvenience, but we've just come back from the forts where the war has kept us busy. It's been over a week since I last set foot in Paris. Welcome to our vigilance committee. I confess that when Citizen Varlin told me that you were passing through the capital and wanted to speak with me, at first I thought it was a joke. Karl Marx, himself, and you his daughter, Jenny! Who could believe it? I am a little surprised. What can I do to help?"

Her voice was calm, even soothing, even though she had just came back from the front. Such composure inspired confidence. Her thin lips barely moved as she spoke, but her words were crystal clear and forceful. She took off her cap, revealing her brown hair pulled back and a slender forehead that gave no indication of her age. Her eyes sparkled with intelligence and her face embodied generosity. I was in awe. Taking Moor off guard, I answered for both of us.

"Quite the opposite! We only wish we could assist you in some way or another. We have come to better understand the impetus of your insurrection in order to provide, as far as possible, the internationalist support that your struggle deserves. We don't want to hold you up for too long from your other responsibilities, but we really wanted to see you. Our friends have told us so much about you."

"I am honored," responded Michel. "But I am only one individual among many of the Commune's fighters. Just a drop of water in a human ocean which, fortunately, is now roaring. Yesterday's mute crowds are speaking out today. You can't help but admire the uprising. The poor who have gone without bread, without clothing, and without shelter are finally joining hands. As you know, carrying the torch of justice is no easy task, but it is indispensable if we are to reach the daylight. Mankind has spent its life in doubt so long that the immense majority don't know their own strength. Today, Paris is populated by those who are hunting the very stars themselves. Believe me, I am nothing, the Commune is everything. It is filled with a multitude of heroes who are writing, through their actions at this very moment, the legends of the times to come. Versailles intends to shatter our dream. But we are waiting for them with determination and our bayonets are ready, held steady in the hands of a whole people like so many ears of corn. And even if they were to exterminate us one by one, they will never be able to murder freedom with shot and cannon. We have broken the chains of a cruel past that has long weighed on our backs. And now that we got a taste of freedom, no man nor woman wants shackles clamped on once more. But first we must win the war if we hope to make our dreams come true. Do you understand, Jenny?"

"Of course," I replied, "especially because the stakes are high. Know that the world is watching you and that many proletarians identify with the fight you are leading. And they see the place women have taken in this uprising. On March 18, your committee's action appeared decisive in starting the revolution itself!"

"In fact, our only contribution was to alert the workers' neighborhoods and to sound the alarm," Michel recalled modestly. "The flood of people who followed inexorably didn't need anyone to lead it in order to overwhelm the entire capital. If women have been the most able to sound the call, it is because we act instinctively, without allowing ourselves to be overwhelmed by political calculations which, by one thousand and one considerations, end up underestimating the immanent spontaneity of the oppressed. The people are fighting resolutely, hoping for nothing in return other than the liberation of all. The old world aimed to make women a caste. The new world brings us together; our goal is to free humanity so that each human being can finally find his own place. On March 18, we were lifted off the ground, and the vanguard was carried to the front by a tide of women. If Versailles had as many enemies among men as it has among women, the reaction would be in deep trouble! Women, the so-called faint of heart, have always known how to say 'We must!', even while we endure pain without hatred, without anger, without pity for ourselves or for others, whether our hearts bleed for them or not."

"How did your movement manage to play such a role?" I asked.

"It took a long time," Michel replied. "Our committee is the political fruit of the years' work preceding the Commune, a period during which Paris was nothing more than revolutionary clubs, political trials, assemblies, and demonstrations. The Commune's lava smoldered underneath the Empire for years before the volcano erupted on March 18. And we were part of the magma from the start, organizing ourselves among women. How could we have done otherwise? The proletarian is nothing but a slave, and a proletarian wife nothing but a slave of a slave."

She uttered this last sentence with a smile that was one part connivance and one part serious. Varlin had told us about her background. In the early 1860s, several teachers, including Michel, began sharing their thirst for ideals and their own freedom every evening during elementary education classes held in a small room on Rue Hautefeuille. Without knowing it, this small group of women would soon take part, in its own way, in a growing tumult shaking French society, simply because they decided to turn their aspirations for social justice into concrete solidarity by offering classes. They first did so in the day school on Rue des Cloÿs in 1865, next at the school on Rue d'Oudot in 1868, and then by founding the democratic workers' aid society the next year. Their involvement was no longer limited to providing free courses at the vocational school on Rue Thévenot; it extended far beyond the confines of schools. Faced with poverty and its ravages, this group of women decided spontaneously to provide assistance for needy children, often orphans. And as they believed that poverty was not innate, the time had come to tackle the root of the problem. One thing led to another and they began interfering in the various cogs of public and democratic Parisian life. This is how we came to find Louise Michel and her friend Marie Ferré participating in all 18th arrondissement political meetings. She had been involved for a long time.

"When did you launch your republican women's citizen vigilance committee?" I inquired.

"Just after the fall of the Empire, mainly to organize concrete solidarity; first, by distributing soup and meals to the poorest people. But we soon ended up participating in everything. The war made us paramedics, and the Commune transformed us into female combatants. And here I am a member of the 61st Montmartre Marching Battalion. In fact, Jenny, we have learned that in order to live you also have to be prepared to die."

Father, who had not yet intervened in the discussion, cleared his throat loud enough to remind us that he was there too.

"Your determination is very heartening. Sincerely. Elisabeth Dimitrieff gave us the same speech yesterday..."

"That's great news then," Michel replied.

"Why do you say that? Did you doubt she would?" asked Moor.

"Not at all. I respect all the women of the Commune, including those of the Place de la Corderie. In particular for this good Madame Lemel from the bookbinders trade union, whose revolutionary La Marmite kitchen prevented so many people from starving during the siege. A real tour de force of dedication and intelligence. My understanding is that the Union des Femmes has been looking to buy guns these days. I fully subscribe to this approach because it will not be enough to sew uniforms for the National Guard, it will be necessary to know how to shoot. I have no doubt that we will find ourselves on the barricades alongside them soon enough."

"What is your analysis of the military situation?" asked Father.

"It is extremely worrying. The Commune's army is no more than a handful compared to that of Versailles. Only our determination and courage have allowed us to hold out for so long. We have very few professional soldiers in our ranks, and we are sorely lacking in experience. Political determination is also lacking. Only an all-out offensive against Versailles can win. We've known that half-measures will do no good since our partial advance failed on April 3. And since April 5, the southern and western batteries—which had been set in place by the Germans during the war against Paris— are now being used by the Versaillese. The Moulineaux redoubt and Fort d'Issy are constantly being taken and then retaken. And there is a perilous line from Asnières all the way to Passy along which the Versaillese attack us day after day. The whole west of the city is constantly being sprayed with bullets, from Porte Maillot to the Champs-Elysées. I saw our soldiers' sacrifices with my own eyes everywhere I went, whether it was on the fortifications, in Issy, at the Clamart train station, or on the Peyronnet de Neuilly barricade. Buildings are gutted, houses in ruins, corpses litter the ground. What desolation. I have seen more young men than I can count cut down by those horrible explosive bullets. I can still picture one unfortunate man who was shot with one such bullet at the heart of the front in the Hautes Bruyères trenches. Our front lines have stood strong, but we have paid with a tragic loss of life. Meanwhile, we are lost in endless discussions in the rear over what powers the Hôtel de Ville's should have. While we are talking about revolution, Versailles is acting, they are waging war on us."

"Revolution and war are basically two sides of the same coin, no?" interjected Father, more as a statement than a question. "The offensive that you are calling for against Thiers's troops on military grounds, an assessment which I fully share, implies the need to seize the Banque de France on political grounds, rather than to negotiate with it, for example?"

"Yes, probably," acknowledged Michel. "Especially since our biggest mistake so far has been failing to plant a stake in the heart of the finance vampire. The Banque de France, that is the real hostage. And there it sits, right under our noses, and we hardly even touch it! How completely do revolution and war merge? That is difficult to estimate. I note that you never tire of wanting to connect contradictions thanks to the miracles of the dialectic. And all of this has its share of truth. Yet some of our endless debates about the future end up paralyzing our actions today. We should have marched on Versailles from the start."

"We absolutely agree on this point and I take nothing away from the importance of winning the fight on all fronts," Father said emphatically. "I hear what you are saying. Especially since you have earned a solid reputation when it comes to fighting a war. The *Cause du peuple* newspaper reported on April 14 that, after having fought valiantly at Les Moulins, you were wounded on Fort d'Issy. Nothing serious I hope?"

"A simple scratch on the wrists. Nothing that deserves such publicity. But I saw disemboweled, mutilated bodies, shattered skulls. So many heroes have died for the cause. You know, rumors are rife, for better or for worse. Versailles claims that I ride in a fancy coach, just because I had to requisition a serviceable carriage for my travels because of an old ankle injury which prevents me from walking. I am not ashamed of who I am, and I sincerely believe I can say that I am not a bad soldier, either."

I listened to this exchange between Father and Louise Michel closely and felt a rush of pride. I had the deepest gratitude for this woman. Her simple explanations spoke to me and her stories fascinated me. So much so that I couldn't help allowing myself a slight digression, which Moor immediately disapproved of with a scowl.

"I'm sorry for this indiscretion," I said, ignoring Father. "But is it true that after the counter-revolutionary demonstration of March 22, you personally tried to kill Thiers in Versailles?"

My transgression of paternal authority made her smile. She answered me, bluntly, in a nostalgic and slightly nonchalant tone.

"Dear Jenny, my Blanquist comrades, Raoul Rigault and Théophile Ferré, succeeded in dissuading me. History will tell if they were right or wrong. However, I couldn't resist the idea of going there, disguised and unrecognizable, to see what the headquarters of the reaction looked like. I was not disappointed! How many horrors and nonsensical lies I heard about us while I was there! One news dealer explained his hatred of the Commune to me, and I took a special pleasure in all the terrible things he had to say about Louise Michel. But I returned to Paris, leaving that monster Thiers to sleep soundly in his bed. To be honest, I'm not too happy about that."

Her last statement left the three of us lost in thought for a few moments before horses whinnying and snorting caught our attention. The commotion was coming from the entrance. Louise Michel immediately opened one of the two large windows in her office. It was her team of horses that was protesting. She issued firm instructions, but did not shout, "Treat the horses right, calm them down, but don't abuse them, you know how much I hate that!"

"Excuse me, my friends," Michel said. "Cruelty to animals repels me in the same way as human suffering. Where were we?"

Father took advantage of the incident to regain control of the conversation and refocus the discussion on the most important matters.

"We were talking about how the Commune's political orientation and its military strategy were probably linked. The prohibition of night work by bakers, cooperatives managed by workers, elections, and elected officials being paid a workers' wages, are not all these measures also ammunition against capital?"

"Yes, of course. And you can add to the list: the abolition of the sale of items from the Mont-de-Piété pawnshops, the abolition of the Catholic Church's budget and confiscation of its property, the end of conscription to the standing army, and pensions for the wounded and their widows. The Commune thirsts for many things, including equality between all people and respect for the inalienable rights of humanity, but it also seeks to share artistic and literary creation and scientific knowledge. The people are eager to escape from the old world, by any exits that may be open to them. Yes, Paris, the capital of mankind, is finally breathing. But Versailles aims to suffocate us again, in a bloodbath if necessary. Our rifles will threaten them far more than our political reforms which, after all, will never see the light of day if we suffer a military defeat."

"It is hard to dispute your argument," concurred Father. "I only wanted to hear your point of view about the unique and innovative aspect of this revolution. It has confounded all the political prognoses we debated within the IWA, no matter what faction—"

"Perhaps because freedom and justice are not a matter of a pre-established program," interrupted Michel. "Blanqui is quite right to say that no intellectual argument can anticipate this type of human creation. At best, we can prepare the cradle of the new world, but no one can foresee or draw up the new world's qualities. Let's make the revolution and then we'll see what comes next. I can still hear him saying, 'Tear down the old society, the new one will be found under the rubble!'"

"Are you a Blanquist yourself?" inquired Moor.

"That's what people say about me. My close friends are, but I am wary of labels. I have the deepest admiration for Blanqui, who we affectionately nicknamed Jailbird after he was sentenced to long years following the failed insurrection of May 12, 1839. I appreciate his brazen determination, unwavering courage, and personal disinterest in institutional intrigue. He taught us to resist, but also taught us that we must want to win the war that the rich launched against the poor long ago. 'Yes, Gentlemen, it is war between the rich and the poor, and it is the rich who started it!' He always repeats this tirelessly. Last August, his supporters attempted to give history a push by proclaiming the Republic without waiting for the Empire to collapse on its own. They just barely missed seizing the weapons at La Villette depot. Émile Eudes, known as 'the General,' and Gabriel Marie Brideau were both condemned to death as a result. However, they were saved in the nick of time by the Napoleon III's defeat by the Germans at Sedan, a defeat that proved fatal to the Empire. Last September, we joined Blanqui in front of the Cherche-Midi prison to welcome them on their release. And on October 31, and again on January 22, we took the plunge together to proclaim the Commune on our own initiative rather than letting the Versaillese attack us first, which is what finally happened in March, sparking the Commune's proclamation. I especially admire Blanqui's voluntarism, a trait for which he has paid dearly."

"There's no doubt about it," replied Father. "His imprisonment has created a gap in the Commune's leadership. I readily admit that if the proletariat has regrouped in recent years around revolutionary socialism and communism, his actions have a lot to do with it. In the eyes of the French bourgeoisie, communism bears the name of Blanqui. However, don't you think that the March

18 uprising has forced us all to readjust our political analyses? The Commune cannot be compared to previous attempts at insurrection. Instead, it is the act of the people and the proletariat themselves, not simply an armed minority ready to overthrow the powers that be. It is living proof that a conscious majority can take charge of society on its own—"

"Does that surprise you?" chided Michel. "Isn't the emancipation of the workers the act of the workers themselves? You know this lovely IWA maxim better than I do, it seems to me—"

"Perhaps some in the IWA have lost sight of this to a certain degree," snapped Father.

"I don't know anything about that, but I will be careful not to pass judgment. Especially since I have always considered the IWA's headquarters at the Maison de la Corderie to be a temple for world peace and freedom. Many comrades are members of the International for this very reason, because it represents, better than any other force, the voice of freedom that has been crisscrossing the globe in recent years, raising demands made by the have-nots across all borders. But I must say that the IWA's perpetual quarrels and the incessant ideological infighting leads me to prefer the more practicable path taken by the revolutionary clubs, the district committees, and those fighting on the ramparts. That is where the fire of revolt by the poor burns like a blazing inferno, far from the endless political debates on the nature of power which, in turn, produce only a lot of smoke."

"The outcome of the struggle, however, partly depends on the outcome of this question," responded Moor. "After all, Blanqui himself has proposed in some of his writings a revolutionary dictatorship. What do you think of that?"

"The dictatorship, whatever that means, seems to me to contradict the universal freedom that we claim for humanity."

"That may be," conceded Father, "but the Commune appears to be an unprecedented form of power, one that seeks to extinguish itself by immediately getting rid of the bureaucratic flaws of the state apparatus."

"A self-extinguishing power?" scoffed Michel. "I doubt there is such a thing."

"Nothing is written in stone," replied Moor, "but I am convinced that the Commune is an important first; its existence represents a seizure of power by the workers themselves. The specific form of emancipation discovered at long last. A few days ago, I wrote to Kugelmann saying that in the last chapter of my *Eighteenth Brumaire of Louis Bonaparte*, I predicted that 'the next attempt of the French revolution will be no longer, as before, to transfer the bureaucratic-military machine from one hand to another, but to smash it.' The state apparatus is a boa constrictor that is suffocating civil society, but the Parisian working class is casting it off."

"You are very optimistic on the subject, my friend," Michel observed. "Power, even our own, even now, brings many more problems than solutions."

"Do you subscribe to the anarchists' arguments?"

"Who knows. I admit I am inclined more toward unlimited freedom than the exercise of power which seems cursed..."

A polite and respectful silence settled between Louise Michel and Moor. Each of them was hardheaded and knew deep down that their discussion had merely defined the extent of the already established agreements and disagreements existing between them. Outside, the crowd was still lively. The Parisian people were determined to keep the Rue de la Chapelle buzzing into the night. Louise Michel paid tribute to this effervescence by reciting a few lines that came to her mind.

> *O people, only you never deceive*
> *When your eye are fixed, and standing on this sacred shore,*
> *Thoughtful, awaiting the hour of your tide to come in.*

"Victor Hugo, right?" queried Father.

"Yes. I never tire of his poems."

Someone then knocked at the door. A woman entered shyly, signaling to Louise Michel. They were asking for her at the committee office. Father got up to put Louise Michel at ease, knowing she had to leave.

"Thank you for your time and also for your frankness. It is an honor to have had the opportunity to share our ideas. The future will settle our differences. Take care and we wish you courage for the struggle that awaits you!"

"Thanks to you both," said Michel. "I am sorry our exchange is ending so quickly. Certainly, my heart and soul are consumed with the action at this time. We will see what tomorrow brings, depending on whether the Commune wins or loses. As for partisan affiliations, we should push them to the background in my opinion. To tell the truth, I do not feel myself belonging to any group. Or maybe I belong to all of them, as long as they attack the accursed edifice of the old society, whether with a pickaxe, a grenade, or fire.

Then she left to join her comrades. Father and I exited through the security perimeter, walking down the Goutte d'Or in search of an omnibus that could take us back to Leo's house. Neither of us dared to speak about the improbable and incredible meeting. Later I wondered if it had really taken place.

8

THE RETURN TO LONDON

On April 19, the weather was very fine. Father wanted to take a walk in the Jardin du Luxembourg, which he had visited often during his stay in Paris in 1843 and 1844. We decided to go on foot, taking Rue de la Glacière and Boulevard de Port-Royal to this magnificent place always full of Parisians eager to breathe in some fresh air. Students from the Latin Quarter, workers from the popular suburbs, and mothers with their children all shared the benches and lawns in a happy mix. The chestnut trees were in bloom and we could hear, here and there, the joyful song of different kinds of birds. Paris in spring is so radiant, we would have liked to stay a few more weeks.

Suddenly, a curious character, half-bourgeois, half-lumpen, approached us and spoke to Moor.

"Excuse me, sir, are you not the German publicist Karl Marx, exiled to London?"

Father replied calmly but firmly: "I'm sorry, sir, but you are mistaken. I don't know what you are talking about. I am an English fabric merchant, visiting France for business."

His English was impeccable, of course, but he spoke with a slight German accent. We took our leave without waiting for an answer.

Back home, Moor reported the incident to Léo, who was quite worried.

"He's probably a snitch, all the scoundrels are working for the Versaillese, sniffing around the streets of Paris."

Father did not seem to attach great importance to our unpleasant encounter. Léo moved on to another topic.

"Our comrade, Auguste Serraillier, the delegate of the International in France, would like to meet you. As you should know, he is the object of vicious slander from Felix Pyat.

"Yes, we discussed it in the General Council and we will publicly denounce Citizen Pyat's cowardly intrigues. This character is one of the loudmouths who, by repeating the same string of clichéd criticisms of the government year after year, pass themselves off as revolutionaries. They are a necessary evil of which we will rid ourselves over time. Hopefully, the Commune will have time to do so.[1] It would give me great pleasure to see Serraillier again."

But the next day, Léo came back very agitated from his work at the Finance Commission.

"The Versaillese are spreading a rumor that the Prussian Red Karl Marx, principal leader of the IWA, is secretly in Paris. They say you are the puppeteer pulling the strings, the leaders of the Commune only obey your orders, they are merely puppets in the service of an international conspiracy. Dear Karl, you are in danger … and so are we. Your presence in Paris has become a threat to your own security as well as the Commune's image. I'm afraid that you must return to London."

Father thought in silence for a few minutes but had to face facts.

---

1 Editors' note: Elected a member of the Commune by the 10th arrondissement, the publicist Felix Pyat, an opponent of the IWA, abstained from taking part in the fighting of May 1871 and fled to England.

"Léo, you're right. We have to go," he concluded. "We will immediately pack our bags. Please let Jean-François know that we will take the boat to Dover which leaves tomorrow at 2 p.m. I would in no way want to harm the Commune by staying here. Regardless, I have gathered a wealth of documentation which will enable me to write my report to the IWA Council. I would have liked to have met up with more friends, our brave Auguste Serraillier, for example. But that would be imprudent, a mistake. We will leave."

We packed quickly and shared one last Parisian meal with Léo, who had prepared beef bourguignon for us, a very French dish, indeed! After the coffee, we finished off our meal with Calvados apple brandy and relaxed in the living room. Moor and I sat on an old, dilapidated but comfortable sofa, and Léo sat in his slightly torn-up armchair, where he spent several minutes filling his pipe with tobacco.

Father and Léo passed the evening discussing the future of the Commune. I was tired and worried but took some notes. My anxiety had as much to do with the uncertain fate of this marvelous revolutionary experience as it did with the threats against Charles, my fiancé.

Léo was concerned with the Versaillese propaganda campaign.

"Thiers and his clique accuse us of 'communism.' How should we respond?"

"Dear Léo, we must make this title our own!" Moor replied excitedly. "The Commune aims to expropriate the expropriators, to transform the means of production, land and capital—which are today nothing more than a means to enslaving labor—into instruments of freely associated labor. Isn't it true that the Commune has supported the creation of cooperatives? And, certainly, if all the cooperative associations were to regulate production according to a common plan, thus placing it under their own control by ousting the capitalist system of property, wouldn't that constitute communism, the so-called 'impossible' communism?"

Léo was listening, but his slight grin suggested he found Moor's argument a bit far-fetched.

"Yes, but we only took a few timid steps, allowing the workers to take over the abandoned businesses—"

"Léo, the Commune's greatest social achievement is its own existence. The particular measures it pursues only indicate the tendencies of a government of the people by the people. It demonstrates its vitality by is very existence and confirms its theory through its actions. Your Commune has taken up the voice of the whole of Europe, not by relying on brute force, but by leading a social movement, by giving substance to the aspirations of the working class in all countries."

"I fully share your point of view," agreed Léo. "It is this emancipatory calling that constitutes the political and moral force of the Paris Commune. But I fear that our military strength, which is by no means imposing, is insufficient in the face of the threat posed by the regular Versaillese army, reinforced by Bismarck's release of the prisoners from the Bonapartist army."

"Of course, you are right," Moor commiserated. "The Paris of the Commune, thinking Paris, working Paris, fighting Paris, the Paris of dreams, radiating enthusiasm for its own historic initiative, giving its all to bring to birth a new society, has almost forgotten the cannibals at its gates! These slave traders in power in Versailles, clinging to this monkey Thiers, plot against the people and dream of crushing the Commune in blood. I share your concerns, my friend. Will the barricades in Paris's streets block the advance of Versailles' guns? Varlin wants to believe that, just like on March 18, some of the regular army's troops will hoist their rifle butts in the air... If Engels were here in my place, he could perhaps have helped you. Our 'General' had prepared a plan to liberate Paris, but it seems that this document has been lost."

It was my turn to speak up.

"The Commune needs all forces available to the Parisian people. It's a shame it won't accept women as combatants. They are not lacking courage and determination."

Father, who rarely contradicts me, warmly supported my point.

"You are a thousand times right, Jennychen!" he practically shouted. "I must say that I was impressed by the Parisian women. Not only thanks to meeting our two admirable revolutionaries Elisabeth Dmitrieff and Louise Michel, but thanks to everything I heard and saw during all our conversations and strolls through insurgent Paris. The women of the Commune are heroic, noble, and devoted, like the women of antiquity. Although they were not admitted to the National Guard, I am convinced that, in this time of danger, many will be found on the barricades."

While taking long puffs of his pipe, Léo raised another subject worrying him.

"The Versailles inner circle accuses the comrades of the International Workingman's Association of secretly leading the Commune, following orders from London. We must disarm this insidious propaganda, which is having a certain influence among the population. What do you think, Karl?"

Father thought for a few moments, considering the best way to respond. Finally, he spoke, with a certain solemnity.

"Léo, on this subject, as on communism, we should not be ashamed of our commitments. We are proud of the eminent role that the Parisian section of the International is playing in this glorious revolution. The flower of the working class of all countries, which adheres to the International and is imbued with its ideas, is naturally found everywhere at the head of revolts of the exploited. In fact, in whatever form, and under whatever circumstances the class struggle takes shape, it is only natural that IWA members should be in the front row. It is rare for someone like Tolain to betray our movement's ideals, and we will undoubtedly exclude him from the International."

Léo listened intently, but I could tell he wasn't exactly pleased with Father's answer.

"I share your pride in seeing our comrades among the Commune's most active combatants. But we must respond to the Versaillese slander, who present us as shadowy conspirators..."

In his response, Moor took the sarcastic tone he adopted whenever he referred to the Versailles "slave traders," as he called them.

"You're right, Leo. Bourgeois understanding, imbued with the spirit of the police, naturally imagines the IWA as a sort of secret conspiracy, whose central authority directs, from time to time, explosions in different countries. These fools imagine that London is giving 'orders' to the Paris section of the International. But all one has to do is quote the International's resolutions prior to March 18 which make it abundantly clear that the IWA's General Council did not foresee, let alone 'lead,' the uprising that established the Commune."

And with that painfully honest conclusion, we said good night. It was late, and the next day was bound to be taxing.

Early in the morning of April 20, Jean-François was waiting for us in his carriage.

"It's a shame you have to leave now," he sighed. "Everything will be decided in the next few weeks. We are going to crush the Versaillese and the Commune will spread over all of France!"

We were far from sharing the enthusiastic optimism of our young friend, but we were careful not to contradict him.

Léo bid us an emotional farewell.

"If we are successful, dear Karl and Jenny, the Commune will invite you to come and live in Paris! And if we perish on the barricades, may the International honor our memory."

"Léo, we hope that the Commune will win," said Father. "However, in case of defeat, remember that your life is precious to us, your friends, but also to the whole International. You must live and continue the fight. If the battle is lost, you must escape the Versaillese and go into exile in London."[2]

The comment clearly was too dark for him to consider. Jean-Francois gave the horses a snap of his whip and the carriage departed. This was the end of our clandestine visit to Paris. Neither Moor nor I will never forget it, but we will keep it a secret.

We arrived in Calais a few hours later. Jean-François left us standing in front of the border post and headed back to Paris after having embraced us very warmly.

"You will be back, I'm sure! You will be guests of the Commune and we will make you honorary citizens of our Social Republic."

"Thank you very much, my dear Jean-François, for your help, your friendship, your enthusiasm!" I replied, overcome with emotion. "With fighters like you, the Commune will be victorious!"

Once the carriage left, we went to the police checkpoint, not being too worried since we had good English passports in the

---

2   Editors' note: Frankel did decide to go into exile, but only after having fought on the Commune's last barricade.

name of John and Sarah Richardson. Fortunately, the sinister Baron Desgarre was not there. The policeman behind the control desk stamped our passports without too much difficulty and returned them to us. However, a few seconds later, something suddenly seemed to spark his memory, and he repeated the name Richardson, Richardson, several times.

"Wait for me here a few minutes, I have to consult my colonel," he ordered and left for another office.

Moor and I looked at each other, taken aback; did he know something? If they discovered Father's identity, he risked ending up like Duval and Flourens, shot without trial.

We were located on the ground floor next to the exit to the control office, which was guarded by an armed enlisted soldier. What to do?

Suddenly, from a distance, we heard the sounds of fighting; apparently two drunken soldiers were getting into it. Our guard left the door and went to the window on the other side of the office to see what was going on. Without hesitation, passports in hand, we headed toward the door, walking calmly but with long strides. We were outside within seconds and quickly made our way to the English boat waiting along the quay.

In less than a minute we climbed the ladder and settled in on the deck of the ship. A few more minutes and the captain ordered his crew to pull up the ladder, weigh anchor, and start up the engines. At that moment, running, and out of breath, the unfortunate policeman from Versailles approached, accompanied by two soldiers. Furious that the ship was leaving, he shouted to the captain.

"We have to get on your ship, a dangerous individual is among your passengers!"

"I'm sorry, sir," replied the captain in English. "This ship, from Her Majesty the Queen of England's navy, is British territory. French police are not admitted."

And for good measure, faced with the police officer's furious gesticulations, he added, "Excuse me sir, but I am already behind my schedule, I have to leave."

And with that, he took off! We were saved.

Onboard, one passenger, bourgeois and philistine to the bone, commented, "Who might this dangerous character be? No doubt one of those Communard assassins! I hope that Thiers settles his score with those scoundrels who dare attack private property and steal money from the Banque de France."

"Don't worry," replied another, "in a few days this affair will be over, and I, for one, hope that the scum will be shot down mercilessly to the last."

We were careful not to intervene in these nauseating conversations.

A few hours later we disembarked in Dover; passport control only took a few minutes and we took a horse-drawn carriage to London. After a brief trip we were back home in Maitland Park where Jenny and Eleanor, surprised and excited, hugged us. We hadn't even had time to tell them we were coming. We recounted our adventures in insurgent Paris in great detail, urging them to keep the trip a secret.

My notebook ends here. I hope it remains the best kept secret in the world.

POSTFACE

The reader will have easily guessed that this is a work of "political fiction" or "imaginary history." As the saying goes, "any resemblance of the events described herein with the actual biography of Marx is purely coincidental." In fact, no coincidence is possible, since the events described herein did not take place. Jenny Marx's marvelous "Blue Notebook" is, like so many other literary "found manuscripts," an invention of the authors.

Why did we choose this literary, not to say romantic, form of expression, this "fictional biography?" The 150th anniversary of the Paris Commune has given rise to a large number of works of an historical or theoretical nature, some of which are of great value. We wanted to do something different, a bit further out, a bit on the fringes, a bit outside of established disciplines and time-honored approaches.

The aim of this unusual form was to bring to life and make tangible, through our imaginations, Karl Marx's passionate interest in the Commune of 1871 and its protagonists, as well as his extraordinary ability to *learn from the event*, a kind of living thought exercise that he would put down on paper in one of his major works, *The Civil War in France*.

The imaginary, sometimes anachronistic, encounters of protagonists who never, in fact, met is a well-established literary technique. In our modest work, we wanted to pay tribute to some of the most endearing figures in this historic and foundational event for the workers' movement.

Using this narrative fiction, we have tried to present their ideas, doctrines, the analyses in the form of dialogues between living people, between singular individuals. As for historical events, we have tried to capture them through the astonished and delighted eyes of our two "visitors."

In the final analysis, the motivation for this attempt is entirely subjective: we wanted to bring these characters together in insurgent Paris! We dreamed up a dialogue between Karl and Jenny and the Communards, and we tried to give shape to our dream through an imaginary story.

ABOUT HAYMARKET BOOKS

Haymarket Books is a radical, independent, nonprofit book publisher based in Chicago. Our mission is to publish books that contribute to struggles for social and economic justice. We strive to make our books a vibrant and organic part of social movements and the education and development of a critical, engaged, international left.

We take inspiration and courage from our namesakes, the Haymarket martyrs, who gave their lives fighting for a better world. Their 1886 struggle for the eight-hour day—which gave us May Day, the international workers' holiday—reminds workers around the world that ordinary people can organize and struggle for their own liberation. These struggles continue today across the globe—struggles against oppression, exploitation, poverty, and war.

Since our founding in 2001, Haymarket Books has published more than five hundred titles. Radically independent, we seek to drive a wedge into the risk-averse world of corporate book publishing. Our authors include Noam Chomsky, Arundhati Roy, Rebecca Solnit, Angela Y. Davis, Howard Zinn, Amy Goodman, Wallace Shawn, Mike Davis, Winona LaDuke, Ilan Pappé, Richard Wolff, Dave Zirin, Keeanga-Yamahtta Taylor, Nick Turse, Dahr Jamail, David Barsamian, Elizabeth Laird, Amira Hass, Mark Steel, Avi Lewis, Naomi Klein, and Neil Davidson. We are also the trade publishers of the acclaimed Historical Materialism Book Series and of Dispatch Books.

ABOUT THE AUTHORS

OLIVIER BESANCENOT was a leading member of the Revolutionary Communist League (LCR) and is one of the founding members of the New Anticapitalist Party in France. He was the LCR candidate for the French presidential election in 2002 and 2007.

MICHAEL LÖWY is emeritus research director at the CNRS (National Center for Scientific Research). His books, including *On Changing the World* and the *Politics of Combined and Uneven Development*, have been translated into twenty-nine languages.

TODD CHRETIEN is the editor of *Eyewitness to the Russian Revolution* and *State and Revolution*. He is also the translator of Michael Löwy's *Revolutions*.

ALSO AVAILABLE FROM HAYMARKET BOOKS

Communist Insurgent: Blanqui's Politics of Revolution
Doug Enaa Greene

How Revolutionary Were the Bourgeois Revolutions?
Neil Davidson

Marx in Soho: A Play on History
Howard Zinn; also on audio CD, performed by Brian Jones

The Paris Commune: A Revolution in Democracy
Donny Gluckstein

Revolutions
Michael Löwy

The Spectre of Babeuf
Ian Birchall

The Women Incendiaries
Edith Thomas

The Women's Revolution: Russia 1905–1917
Judy Cox